Meet the soldiers of the Military K-9 Unit series and their brave K-9 partners

Officer: Rachel Fielding

K-9 Partner: Stryker the German shepherd

Assignment: Protect her young niece from her dangerous father with the help of her military veterinarian boss.

Officer: Jacey Burke

K-9 Partner: Greta the Belgian Malinois

Assignment: Stay one step ahead of the killer who's threatening her—without falling for her childhood friend and fellow officer.

Valerie Hansen was thirty when she awoke to the presence of the Lord in her life and turned to Jesus. She now lives in a renovated farmhouse in the breathtakingly beautiful Ozark Mountains of Arkansas and is privileged to share her personal faith by telling the stories of her heart for Love Inspired. Life doesn't get much better than that!

Laura Scott is a nurse by day and an author by night. She has always loved romance and read faith-based books by Grace Livingston Hill in her teenage years. She's thrilled to have published over twelve books for Love Inspired Suspense. She has two adult children and lives in Milwaukee, Wisconsin, with her husband of thirty years. Please visit Laura at laurascottbooks.com, as she loves to hear from her readers.

MILITARY K-9 UNIT CHRISTMAS

VALERIE HANSEN
LAURA SCOTT

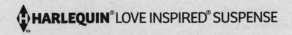
HARLEQUIN® LOVE INSPIRED® SUSPENSE

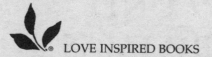

LOVE INSPIRED BOOKS

Recycling programs for this product may not exist in your area.

ISBN-13: 978-1-335-49076-6

Military K-9 Unit Christmas

Copyright © 2018 by Harlequin Books S.A.

Special thanks and acknowledgment are given to Valerie Hansen and Laura Scott for their contribution to the Military K-9 Unit series.

The publisher acknowledges the copyright holders of the individual works as follows:

Christmas Escape
Copyright © 2018 by Harlequin Books S.A.

Yuletide Target
Copyright © 2018 by Harlequin Books S.A.

Printed in U.S.A.

CONTENTS

CHRISTMAS ESCAPE

Valerie Hansen

May God bless the men and women serving in our current military and those whose sacrifices in the past have kept us free. We are grateful beyond words.

And the light shineth in darkness...
–John 1:5

ONE

"I love my job," Rachel Fielding murmured, smiling. "Who wouldn't? I help brave members of the military and get all the free kisses from them I want." She chuckled and blushed, checking her surroundings to make sure no one had overheard her silly musings.

Her patients might have four paws and wagging tails, but they were the dearest part of her job as a veterinary assistant. Sure, some could be hard to handle, but very few had proved impossible in the years she'd worked at Canyon Air Force Base in Texas. Since a blissful marriage and raising her own children didn't seem to be in her future, she'd fill that void via her job. Thankfully, any time she got in a bind trying to tend to a sick or injured dog she could always count on fellow techs or Captain Kyle Roark, DVM, her boss for two of the past four years.

Rachel knelt to hug Stryker, a three-legged German shepherd who had had his front leg amputated after being wounded overseas. For a tough K-9 soldier who had taken down the worst of the worst in battle, he sure was a sweetie—once you gained his trust as she had.

The abrupt opening of a nearby door made them both jump. "Easy, boy," Rachel said to soothe the dog. She

smiled up at her boss. "I'll be in soon. I was just social-
izing Stryker a little on my break."

Captain Kyle Roark shook his head. "It's not that,
Fielding. There's a personal call for you. They say it's
important."

"Sorry." Rachel got to her feet. Since her K-9 buddy
immediately started leaning against her, looking up and
pleading with his beautiful brown eyes, she asked, "Can
I bring Stryker with me? You said he needs more casual
exposure."

"Fine." Roark held the door open for them. "Take your
call on the phone in my office."

"Thanks." Barking echoed in waves along the corri-
dors when Rachel and the big shepherd passed by. Now
that winter had brought a cooldown, the dogs housed at
the training facility and animal hospital were more active
as well as vocal. "Did the caller say what this was about?"

The captain paused at the entrance to his small office
and gestured instead of replying. To Rachel's surprise he
followed her and the dog in, pulled out a chair and said,
"Sit," as he handed her the portable telephone from his
desk. "Please."

Both she and the obedient K-9 complied. Rachel was
getting uneasy. Captain Roark had always been a perfect gentleman with all the enlisted personnel but he had
never, in her memory, acted so solicitous. Her hands were
trembling and she used them both to grip the phone.

"This is Airman Fielding speaking."

A woman's voice captured and held her attention. "I'm
with Patient Services at Municipal Hospital in San Antonio. I have had a terrible time locating you, Ms. Fielding. Is your first name Rachel and do you have a sister,
Angela?"

"Yes. But I haven't seen…"

"Angela is here with us. She's asking for you, Ms. Fielding."

The unspoken meaning behind that statement weighed on Rachel's heart as if a boulder lay atop her chest, making it hard to breathe. Stryker sensed her tension and pressed his good shoulder to her knee. "My sister? Are you sure?"

"Yes, ma'am. If it's at all possible, I urge you to get here immediately."

"Angela's sick?"

"She's been injured. I'm not authorized to go into detail. Everything will be clear once you've visited and spoken with her. You are coming?"

"Of course." Rachel's stomach knotted, and she tasted bile on her tongue. If her sister had been hurt in an accident there would be no reason to keep that information private. Therefore, there was a very good chance Angie's live-in boyfriend was to blame. The mere thought of having to face that horrible man again gave Rachel discernible tremors. She had to ask, "Is her, I mean, is a guy named Peter VanHoven with her?"

"I'm sorry, I have no idea. I was told to contact you and relay your sister's message, that's all."

"All right. Where do I need to go?"

The patient services spokesperson was in the middle of giving directions when Rachel realized she hadn't taken in anything. "Wait. Please. I need…" With that she passed the phone to her captain.

Kyle Roark rose from his perch on the edge of his desk and circled it, picked up a pen and made notes. "Yes, I have it. Thank you. When are visiting hours?"

Although Rachel couldn't hear the other end of the conversation, she read empathy and concern in the veterinarian's expression. His dark eyes were resting on her as he nodded and said, "Yes. I see. All right. Tell her sister that Rachel is on her way." He glanced at his wristwatch. "We should be there before fifteen hundred hours. Thank you."

She stood as he ended the call, using the arm of the chair for added balance. "I'll need to get permission to leave the base and be gone for who knows how long. And I'll need to borrow a car."

"Leave that to me. When you put Stryker back in his kennel, tell Sylvia to cover your duties while I make a few calls and adjust staffing." He was stripping off his white lab coat to reveal a light blue shirt beneath.

Rachel was almost to the door when Roark stopped her by calling out, "Fielding. Change into the civvies you keep in your locker and grab a warm jacket in case we're still gone after sunset. I'm going to contact my commanding officer, Lieutenant General Hall, and explain the emergency situation so there won't be any misunderstandings about both of us being away."

"Are you sure you want to do this?"

"Absolutely. You're clearly in no shape to drive and I'm escorting you to the hospital to see your sister. Period."

"It's very kind of you to offer, Captain."

"You're welcome, Rachel. And please remember to call me Kyle while we're away from the base."

"Of course… Kyle."

"Get going. We need to hit the road in minutes, not hours."

"On my way." So many poignant memories were whirling through Rachel's mind as she changed into jeans, a T-shirt and a lightweight jacket that she hardly gave thought to anything but her sister.

Angela. Dear, sweet, clueless Angela. What a waste her life had been after she'd fallen for Peter. He'd been bad news from the beginning but Angie would never listen, never see him for what he really was: a mean, ruthless bully with a temper to match.

The difference between that man's psyche and that of the trained attack dogs in their program was self-control. A K-9 could be called off by his handler. Once Peter lost his temper and began to inflict suffering, there was no stopping him until he was physically spent. She knew him well. She'd been on the receiving end of his wild temper and vindictive actions more than once.

The price she'd paid had been high. He had cost her the only family she had left in the world.

Kyle drove his military SUV as fast as the speed limit allowed, plus a tad more. The caller from the hospital had not minced words once Rachel had handed him the phone. Her sister was in critical condition with broken bones and a damaged heart and might not live long. He knew what it was like to be cheated of a chance to say goodbye. To express love and devotion one last time. He'd been too late to kiss his wife or his little girl and it still galled him, especially at this time of the year. Sadly, the anniversary of their deaths coincided with Christmas celebrations that were supposed to be joyous.

Well, they sure weren't happy times for him. Not anymore. He didn't try to fake it, either. There was no sense pretending to be having a good time when he wasn't. He didn't expect others to stop enjoying themselves, but he made it clear he did not want to be included. When Christmas Day arrived he was more than willing to take over kennel duties and give most of his enlisted staff the day off. No longer having a family of his own hurt worse on that particular day than at any other time.

Rachel said very little as they drove. Kyle saw her

tense against the seat belt and pull her purse into her lap
as he wheeled into the hospital parking lot and stopped.
Before he could walk around to open the passenger-side
door, she was out and jogging toward the front entrance.
"Wait."

Rachel didn't even bother to shake her head; she simply kept going, making Kyle wonder if she'd heard him.
He'd seen plenty of shocked reactions demonstrated by
both humans and K-9s who had been traumatized in battle, and that was exactly how his vet tech was behaving.
She was trapped in a zone between fight and flight, determination and panic, and that conflict had rendered her
temporarily deaf and mute.

Catching up as she passed through the automatic-
entry doors into the lobby, Kyle caught hold of her arm.
She wheeled, wild-eyed, as if his touch was an attack.

He immediately released her, palms facing out, hands
raised. "Simmer down. They told me your sister is in
the ICU on the fourth floor." He pointed. "Elevators are
over there."

Rachel stared at him for a moment before he saw recognition light her blue eyes. "O-okay. Hurry."

"You need to act calm even if you don't feel it. The
last thing your sister needs is to see you in hysterics."
Kyle pushed the up button for the elevators. "Take some
slow, deep breaths and get it together. What's got you
so spooked?"

"You wouldn't understand." The elevator doors
swished open. Rachel jumped on ahead of him, faced
front and repeatedly punched the button for the fourth
floor.

"Try me." He noticed she was focused not on him, but
on the narrow slice of lobby she could see behind him.

Worry masked her usually sweet expression, and panic dampened the spark in her eyes.

When she slammed the heel of her hand against the control panel, Kyle cautioned again. "Whoa. Beating those buttons to death won't make them work any faster, you know."

"We have to go! Now." She was leaning to one side for a final glimpse as the doors slid smoothly closed. "I think I just spotted Peter."

Whirling, Kyle took a defensive stance, but it was too late. The elevator was moving. "The guy you asked about on the phone? Why didn't you say so?"

"It was just for a second. This guy was wearing a black T-shirt, jacket and a baseball cap so I couldn't see if his long hair was pulled back, but everything about him fit what I remember."

Her lower lip quivered when her gaze met Kyle's. "What am I going to do? I want to be brave for Angie's sake but the thought of facing that man makes me sick to my stomach. She must be in terrible shape to take the chance of sending for me."

Take the chance? The more he learned, the less he liked it. "Why were you and your sister estranged?"

"It's complicated. We don't have time for the whole story."

"Okay, fill me in later. Right now, the important thing is your reunion. Obviously, she wants to make peace or she wouldn't have asked for you. So, make the best of it."

The shiny metal doors slid open on their floor. Rachel stepped into the hallway, looked around and froze.

Kyle placed his hand lightly at her waist. "You can do this. Come on. ICU is this way."

She didn't move. "What if...? What if I was right and

I did see Peter? He can be violent and he could be right behind us."

"If he is, I'll take care of him."

"You'll watch my back?"

"Of course. When you and your sister want privacy, just say the word and I'll step outside."

"Outside the room, maybe. Not outside the hospital. Not that far away. Promise?"

"I promise," Kyle said, frowning.

Rachel blinked back tears. "I wish we had brought Stryker or another K-9 for self-defense. Peter VanHoven is more than Angela's significant other. He's also a sadist with a hair-trigger temper. I'm positive he's the reason she's in intensive care. If he is around here we won't want to cross his path."

"You're that scared of him?"

"Let's just say I've experienced Peter's foul moods firsthand. And I have the scars to prove it."

"I'll stick close." Kyle had already been entertaining an urge to protect and shelter her. Now, it blossomed. It had been a long time since he'd allowed himself to feel proprietary toward any woman, let alone a beautiful one. Why had he failed to notice how truly attractive this vet tech was before?

Kyle's cheeks flamed. That kind of thinking made him decidedly uncomfortable. Rachel Fielding had always acted as if she was just as determined as he was to remain unattached. That constant standoffishness had puzzled him from time to time, but he hadn't questioned her because he was comfortable with it. Now that he'd seen how afraid she was to face her sister's boyfriend, her attitude was beginning to make perfect sense. The man had physically and emotionally injured Rachel in the past and now her poor sister was hurt, too. That was totally unacceptable.

Confounded by his innermost thoughts, Kyle clenched his fists as they made their way down the hallway. A part of him was wishing they would run into this Peter guy so he could tell him off—or more. It wasn't an exemplary Christian attitude, but it certainly was human.

On alert, Kyle stood taller and braced himself to repel the unknown. No low-life abuser was going to get his hands on Rachel without going through him first.

TWO

Keeping watch behind and to the sides, Rachel let Kyle request admittance to the sealed-off ward via the intercom. Automatic doors swished open and her senses were assailed by pungent medicinal smells, beeping machines and an atmosphere so hushed, so heavy, it seemed tangible. If she had not yearned so strongly to be reunited with Angela, she would have turned and fled.

Up ahead, a woman wearing a mask, gloves and a long-sleeved disposable smock gestured to them and pointed. "Ms. Fielding is in the last bed in this row. Behind that curtain. We don't usually allow more than one visitor at a time and a neighbor brought her daughter to see her, but under these circumstances you can go ahead, too."

The extra strength Rachel needed came from the man beside her. She took a deep breath, steeled herself for what she might see and started forward. Off on her left and right, other patients were clearly struggling to survive. Most were elderly, but not all. Angela was barely thirty. This was so unfair.

As they drew closer, Rachel could hear a woman speaking to a child behind the partially drawn curtain next to Angela's bed. When Rachel reached out and pulled it aside with a trembling hand, the sight of her sister's swollen, bruised face and emaciated arms made her gasp. Tears immediately blurred her vision. She rushed forward as an older woman carrying a little girl backed away to make room.

"You came," Angela whispered.

"Of course I did."

"I was afraid you might not."

Previously unshed tears began to slide silently down Rachel's cheeks and she noted that her sister was also weeping. What could she do or say to help? Fond memories made her revert to a long-unused quip. "I had to see my favorite sister."

To Rachel's delight, the comment brought a slight smile to the badly beaten face. "I'm your only sister."

"Picky, picky." Rachel's hands were clasping Angela's on the side of the bed opposite the IV, and she could feel bones inside the painfully thin fingers. Beeping from a nearby machine increased in frequency, and she realized she was hearing her sister's racing pulse.

Slowly, tenderly, Rachel reached to smooth Angela's damp hair off her forehead. "Take it easy, sis. You need to rest so you can get better and take care of your daughter. This pretty little girl must be Natalie."

"Yes. Natalie, this is your aunt Rachel. Maria Alvarez is my neighbor. She's the one who called the police when I couldn't."

Not only did Angela's weeping continue, she looked past Rachel and the others to focus on Kyle. "You're her friend?"

"Kyle Roark. We work together," he said.

"But you are friends, too?" She kept struggling to control her emotions enough to speak.

Rachel answered for him. "Yes. Kyle and I are friends. He drove me here."

"He'll stay?"

That question made Rachel stiffen and peer behind her. "I thought I saw Peter downstairs. Is he…?"

Attempting to shake her head, Angela winced in pain. "He's in jail. The police arrested him for doing this to me."

"Thank God for answered prayers," Rachel confessed. "He's the last person I want to run into. Ever."

"That makes two of us," her older sister admitted, sniffling and struggling to go on. "I'm so sorry, sis. I should have listened to you and left him years ago."

"That's all in the past." Rachel stroked Angela's forehead again. "Right now, you need to worry about getting better."

Again, Angela focused on Kyle, then looked to Mrs. Alvarez. "Maria, can you and this gentleman take Natalie for ice cream or something? Please? I want to talk to my sister. Alone."

"*Sí.*" The full-bodied woman lowered the child to the ground and clasped one of Angela's hands. "Hold on to Senor Kyle, too, Natalie. We don't want him to get lost."

The child complied, slipping her small hand into Kyle's and holding tight, then looking up at him in awe. "He's real big."

Rachel smiled and almost chuckled until her niece added, "I think he could beat up my daddy if he had to."

Rachel's heart clenched. *Of course.* Angela wouldn't be the only victim of her live-in's temper. Peter would have lashed out at anyone who displeased him. The way he had at Angela. And the way he had at her when he'd driven her out of her sister's life that last time.

Returning her full attention to her weeping sibling,

Rachel tried to apologize. "I'm so sorry. I should have found the courage to stay with you."

"Nonsense." Sniffle. "You begged me to go away with you and I was too stubborn and stupid to listen. That's not your fault."

"I wrote. You never answered."

"I couldn't. I just couldn't admit what a horrible mistake I'd made. By the time I thought I was ready to leave Peter I'd lost touch with you."

"You knew I was close by."

"Not for sure. I'd had your unlisted cell number in my phone but Peter took it away. When your letters stopped coming I figured you had washed your hands of me."

"No way. I didn't stop trying to keep in touch," Rachel vowed. "He must have intercepted my letters. I was only writing once a month or so after the first year. It would have gotten easier for him to destroy your personal mail before you saw it."

Falling silent, Angela seemed to struggle to breathe.

"Do you want me to call a nurse?"

"No. No. Just give me a second." She inhaled a little more deeply, wincing and groaning as her chest expanded. "I want you to promise me something."

Rachel leaned closer. "Of course. Anything."

"I want you to take Natalie, look after her and tell her about me so she remembers and knows I loved her."

"I'll be glad to babysit. You can tell her you love her, yourself."

"Promise."

"All right. I promise."

Shuddering, Angela tightened her grip on Rachel's hand. "Don't let Peter get his hands on her, whatever you do."

"How can I prevent it? He's her father."

"Not legally. I never put a father's name on her birth certificate, and we never married. Besides, I have high hopes he'll rot in jail after doing this to me."

"From your lips to God's ears," Rachel quoted, meaning every word. "Is it all right if I take her to the base with me while you're recuperating? I can't be away from my duties too long, and there's a good preschool there for when I'm working."

"Did you take that veterinary aide course you kept dreaming about?"

"Yes. Kyle's the head vet in the military K-9 training program at Canyon Air Force Base and I'm one of his techs. That's what he meant when he said we worked together, although actually I work for him."

Angela managed a lopsided smile. "Wonderful. You'll be with all those protective dogs they train. Couldn't be better."

"And when you get well we'll find you an apartment close to Canyon so we can see each other all the time."

The dreamy, weary expression on her sister's face comforted Rachel. When Angela closed her eyes and sighed, she did the same. Hands still clasped together, Rachel began to pray with her and for her. "Thank you, Father, for healing old wounds in our hearts and for the healing You are about to do in Angela's body. Amen."

Rachel watched Angela's eyelids flutter. Her breathing had been noisy all along but now it began to sound labored even though the beeping machines kept up their even cadence. Rachel wanted to tell Angela how much she loved her but was hesitant to disturb her further. Time ticked past so slowly that every second felt as if it lasted minutes.

Praying silently, Rachel listened to the mechanical manifestations of her sister's life until suddenly Angela was squeezing her hand. Rachel met her gaze, mirrored Angela's smile and felt her heart breaking. An amazing peace and release settled over the bruised face. Angie's pain and suffering were over. Her sister was finally free. Peter couldn't hurt her anymore.

But what about Natalie? The little girl had never met her aunt Rachel before today and now she was going to have to take her away from the only home she'd ever known. How could she possibly make a child understand and accept the situation when she hardly could herself?

Three ICU nurses and a doctor had finished confirming Rachel's fears and had left by the time she heard the sound of boots on the bare floor. Kyle was back. And Natalie was undoubtedly with him. Angela was positioned as if asleep, but Maria Alvarez guessed what had happened in their absence and gasped, beginning to mutter a prayer as she stepped ahead to block Natalie's view.

Kyle, too, quickly closed the distance. He stopped behind Rachel and laid a hand of comfort on her shoulder. "I'm so sorry."

Without hesitation she accepted his condolences by placing one of her hands atop his and saying, "Thank you."

"I wanna see my mama," the little girl whined. She was trying to wiggle past the adults.

"Let her come closer," Rachel said, surprised at how calm and in control she felt despite everything. She held out her hands and Natalie let her pick her up. The urge to kiss the child's hair and stroke her back as a mother would surged through Rachel and squeezed her heart. "I'll take care of you now, honey. You can come and live with me."

The big blue eyes, lashes wet with tears, looked up at Rachel as if she had just promised the world. "I—I don't have to go back to Peter?"

Rachel pulled her close again and dried her cheeks. "No, baby, no. We're not going to have anything more to do with Peter. I promise."

As she comforted her niece and glanced at the others, she saw concern in Maria's expression and disbelief in Kyle's.

"What else can I do?" she asked him aside. "If I send Natalie with Maria, Peter will know how to find her and try to take her back. I have as much legal right to her as he does."

"How do you figure?"

"Angela said they never married and his name is not on the birth certificate. He'd have to go to court to prove he actually is her father, and I'm sure a background check will show him as an unsuitable parent."

"Then we should call the authorities and do this the right way, the legal way," Kyle warned. "You can get in a lot of trouble if you just walk off with her."

"I know, but..." Rachel looked to Maria for moral support and found the older woman staring out the window at the parking lot below. Nobody could blame her for turning away. She'd been sucked into this mess by being a Good Samaritan and probably feared and hated Peter VanHoven almost as much as Angela had.

"Ai-yi-yi." Hands clamped over her mouth, Maria whirled. Rachel tensed. "What is it? What's wrong?"

"It's him! Look. He's coming!"

"Who? Peter? Where?" Rachel asked, joining her. "Angie said he was in jail. Are you sure?"

Kyle crowded closer, too. "Which one is he?"

Maria pointed. "There. Getting out of the old red truck. See?"

"Maybe he's out on bail. If he's the guy I think you mean, he's good and mad. Look at his body language."

"Yeah." Putting Natalie down, Rachel began to gather up the few personal items Maria had brought for the child.

Kyle frowned. "What are you doing?"

She paused only long enough to glance his way and say, "Running. Far and fast."

"That's wrong." Arms folded across his broad chest, Kyle stood like a sentinel, apparently ready to enforce his opinion.

"I don't care if you go with us or not. Natalie and I are leaving."

"Get a grip and think," Kyle urged. "Where will you go?"

"Back to the base if we're welcome to ride with you," Rachel shot back. "Out the door and into hiding if you don't help us. I'm not staying here where VanHoven can get his filthy hands on me or anybody else." She glanced at the still figure on the bed. "He's done enough damage for a lifetime."

Rachel was ready to abandon Kyle and carry out her threat, and she would have, if Natalie had not grabbed a bedraggled baby doll in one hand and Kyle's index finger in the other. The man's expression froze for an instant, then melted in a way Rachel had not seen in the two years she'd worked for him.

He was going to help them escape. She could tell that as surely as if he had spoken.

One final peek out the window was all she allowed herself. No sign of Peter! He must already be passing beneath the entrance canopy, on his way to berate Angie for his arrest when she was the true victim. Rachel had seen it before, plenty of times. It was his excuse for normal.

And since Angie was not going to be available to listen to his tirade, he was sure to turn his wrath on whoever happened to be close by, such as his daughter. Or Rachel. As much as she would like to see someone give him a taste of his own medicine, she knew better than to place Kyle in such a tenuous situation when a confrontation could be avoided.

What she must do is grab her niece and run. Now.

THREE

Rachel sidled through the door from the ICU into the hallway. She had shouldered Natalie's small bag along with her own purse and was towing the child by the hand. Kyle brought up the rear.

Suddenly, Natalie was pulled away. Rachel whirled, ready to do battle, when she realized that her companion had picked up the little girl and was headed in a different direction. For a few seconds she wondered if his plan was to return the child to her father. Then, he allayed her fears.

"Not the elevator, Rachel. He'll probably come up that way. We'll take the stairs. Follow me."

That logic was unquestionable. She fell in behind him. He shouldered through the stairway exit door and cradled Natalie while he waited for Rachel to pass. Her body was trembling, her legs unsteady. Each downward step brought her closer to escape, closer to the parked SUV that would carry them all away before it was too late.

Would they make it? They had to, for Natalie's sake if for no other reason. Rachel had vowed to protect her niece, and that was exactly what she intended to do. Peter was never going to get his hands on her as long as one Fielding sister was left.

She heard the measured thuds of Kyle's boots on the stairs behind her. He was sticking close. Praise the Lord she hadn't made this trip to see Angela alone! A sense of divine presence and peace flooded through her. The fear she had defined as a personal weakness her heavenly Father had used for her good. If her pride hadn't gotten in the way, she might have recognized the hidden blessing sooner.

Their path took them to a side door. Rachel glanced over her shoulder to ask, "Now what?"

"We can circle around or I can bring the truck to you, depending on whether or not this Peter guy spots you. If he came inside the way I suspect, we can make a run for it together."

"Okay."

She started to lean on the push bar to the exterior door as she heard Kyle shout, "No!"

It was too late. A claxon horn was blasting and warning bells sounded. Rachel immediately realized her error. That door was supposed to stay closed and she'd triggered an alarm.

Frustrated, fearful and more angry with herself than anyone else, Rachel faced him with a grimace. "You said we were going to circle around so I thought…"

"Inside, not out there," he shot back. "Come on. Follow me before the guards catch us."

Rachel didn't argue. They turned back into the hallway. Curious employees and patients glanced at them in passing, but nobody approached with questions.

"Walk calmly and slowly," Kyle ordered. "Don't hurry and don't look back. Pretend you think that noise is a nuisance the way everybody else does."

"Okay."

"And stay close. We want to look like a normal family."

Rachel could see wisdom in his suggestion even if heeding it did place her in an awkward position. Putting aside her personal misgivings, she moved to Kyle's side and slipped her hand through the crook of his bent elbow.

That touch was a mistake. His arm was muscular beneath his sleeve, his countenance commanding and sturdy as well as comforting. She knew his hands were especially skillful because she'd watched him do delicate surgeries, but nothing had prepared her for this potent an assault on her senses.

Distracted by the masculine presence beside her, she almost missed spotting a familiar figure fidgeting in front of a bank of elevators.

"Stop," she hissed, giving his arm a tug.

Kyle halted. "What is it?"

"There. Up ahead. See the scruffy man with a pony-tail, cutoffs, bomber jacket and flip-flops by the elevators? That's him. We got here too soon."

"It's still better than coming face-to-face when those doors open upstairs."

"Right." Slinking backward into a shallow doorway, Rachel was relieved when Kyle turned and handed her Natalie.

"Hold her tight and stay behind me so he won't spot you if he looks this way."

"Gladly." Rachel couldn't tell whether the elevator had come and gone until Kyle told her. "The coast is clear. Remember, act normally."

Rachel huffed. "I doubt I'd recognize *normal* if it walked up and bit me in the leg. The only part of my life that ever seemed well ordered was my time in the air force working with K-9s. I can hardly wait to get back on base."

As he ushered her and Natalie toward the automated

sliding doors leading to the parking lot, Kyle was shaking his head. "I'm afraid that by the time you get through all the red tape involved in gaining legal custody of your niece, nothing will feel the same. Not even life on Canyon."

A childish, barely audible "What's that?" sounded in Rachel's ear.

"Canyon Air Force Base," she told the child. "That's where I live."

"Do you have toys?" the wan little voice asked right before a big yawn.

"Well, we have what Senora Alvarez brought for you and there's a wonderful store where we can buy more."

"I don't wanna leave my mama," Natalie whined, rubbing her eyes with her little fists.

"I know you don't, sweetheart. I don't want to leave your mom, either, but we have to go before Peter sees us."

Thin arms tightened around Rachel's neck, reminding her that she had just accepted an immense responsibility, one she was far from certain she was ready for. Suppose her efforts at parenting failed? Or suppose Peter won in court and she had to give Natalie back to him?

That possibility was so unacceptable it brought tears to her eyes. *No, no, no.* She would not fail. She would never give up no matter who or what came against her. She couldn't disappoint her sister—or the frightened child now clinging to her. No matter what happened she was going to stick it out. To win. There was no acceptable alternative.

Glaring sunshine barely warmed the winter day. Kyle loaded the sleepy little girl and her scarce personal belongings into the second seat of the SUV, then began to adjust her seat belt before fastening it. "She should have a booster seat, too, but this will have to do."

"Not if it isn't safe. I hadn't thought about how she was going to ride with us."

Seeing Rachel's tears begin to glisten, Kyle said, "Look. A lot has happened already and I know you're not thinking clearly. That's where I come in. Trust me. I've got this."

Shoulders sagging, Rachel nodded. "I know. I just feel so confused. I'd finally reconciled with my sister and now she's gone again. It's like I was robbed. Twice." She draped her jacket over Natalie to serve as a blanket before sliding into the front passenger seat.

Kyle fought to keep from identifying too closely with Rachel's plight. It was no use. And, considering how bereft she seemed, he figured he owed it to her to commiserate. "I do understand, believe me. It's hard. Any unexpected loss is, especially when it's a younger person."

She sighed. "I really did love my sister even if we hadn't had contact during the past six years. I keep wondering if things would have been different if I'd stayed with her instead of letting Peter scare me off."

"Sure. Maybe he'd have beaten you senscless, instead."

Kyle noted her sidelong glance at the second seat as he started the vehicle, and toned down his responses, beginning with, "Sorry." He started to back out of the parking space. "How much do you know about the whole home situation?"

"Not a lot beyond what I witnessed years ago. Angela managed to tell me some things but it's probably not enough to get him thrown back in jail. At least not until the forensic report is in."

He knew she was purposely being evasive by not mentioning a medical examiner. Surely anyone who had been so severely beaten and had named her attacker on her deathbed would be believed. The problem was whether or not this Peter guy was going to accept any legal edict. Even if he wasn't put in prison for killing Rachel's sister, he should never gain custody of the sweet little girl nodding off in the back seat.

"We can take her home to your apartment and look over what she brought with her. Then I'll go down to the base exchange and buy whatever else she needs."

"You don't have to do that."

"I know." Backing out, he joined a line of cars waiting to leave the lot.

"Then, why?"

"Let's just say it's the right thing for me to do and I don't mind a bit. Okay?"

"Sure. I get it. I have the Christmas spirit, too."

Kyle's head snapped to the side. "Who said anything about Christmas?"

"I'm sorry. I thought, since there are decorations hanging from every lamppost and store windows are all lit up for the holidays, that was influencing you."

"Well, it isn't." His hands had fisted on the steering wheel so firmly his knuckles were turning white.

Her voice was soft, tender. "I understand completely."

"What do you mean?" There was no way she could know his story without digging into his past. He'd been very careful to keep his history to himself after selling his civilian practice and reenlisting as an air-force veterinarian.

"Holidays can be tough on everybody," Rachel said. "There really are no perfect family gatherings or ideal celebrations. After my parents died, Christmas was never the same, even when Angela and I tried to make it festive." She took another peek at the snoozing little girl before she added, "That was before Peter came on the scene, of course. Once he and Angie were a couple, we didn't even try. And now…"

"Okay. One thing at a time," Kyle said, purposely changing the subject. "Do you have a place for her to sleep? Enough food in the house? Blankets, pillows, that kind of thing?"

"Yes. She'll need some decent clothes for preschool if there isn't anything suitable with her. And probably shoes. Those flip-flops aren't going to be warm enough." Slowly shaking her head, Rachel made a face. "I don't imagine she's used to having much, given the way she looks today."

"According to what Senora Alvarez told me when we went to the cafeteria, your sister had a rough time. So did Natalie."

"Undoubtedly. My biggest concern isn't her past—it's her future. How am I going to keep Peter away from her?"

"Once we're on the base it will be relatively safe." The line of cars was moving too slowly to suit Kyle, but since it was almost his turn at the exit he tamped down his anxiety.

Rachel cited recent history. "Oh, really? Look what that serial killer Boyd Sullivan did. He sneaked on and off base for months before he was caught. If he could do it, so can Peter."

"Sullivan was a special case. He was a certified nutjob. Those are unpredictable."

"And Peter isn't?" Her volume increased on the final word.

"Shush. You'll wake Sleeping Beauty."

"She is beautiful, isn't she?" Rachel's smile was so tender as she gazed at the napping little girl that Kyle's heart clenched almost as tightly as his fists. Visions of another little girl, of his precious Wendy, melded with the current image of Natalie and gave him a jolt. He hadn't been there for his own daughter or for his wife when they'd needed him, and that failure had eaten away at him for four long years.

Was God giving him a second chance to protect an innocent little girl who had no other champion? Perhaps, but the opportunity was bittersweet. How much better it would have been if his little family had never been torn apart by that drunk driver in the first place.

And how much more he would have trusted in his Christian faith if his prayers for their survival had been answered that awful winter night. He hadn't wanted to let them go, to lose them forever, yet he had. It had been a terrible struggle to go on without them, to accept his loneliness and live with it. He'd made a new life by returning to the air force, where he knew he could do the most good, and had kept his emotional distance from fellow officers as well as the enlisted personnel assigned to him. Until now.

Kyle knew he was entering uncharted territory and his misgivings were almost strong enough to cause him to back off. Almost. But not quite.

His innermost thoughts were directed to God while he continued to fidget and inch the SUV forward in line. *Why, God? And why at Christmastime? You know how this hurts so why a woman and little girl? And why me?*

He didn't need an audible reply to know the answer. The trauma of the past made him particularly suited to this task. He had lost to evil once by not being totally diligent, not making himself available when his gut told him he should. It would not happen again. No matter what developed in regard to his vet tech and her niece, he was going to be there for her. For them.

He would not make the same mistake twice.

A horn honked behind them as the space at the very front of the line was vacated. Rachel jumped at the noise. So did Kyle. Checking for cross traffic on the street, he also glanced toward the hospital and caught his breath.

"Rachel," he said abruptly. "Look over there. Is that…?"

She followed Kyle's gaze, then immediately whirled to face him. Her complexion paled and her lips parted. She didn't have to speak to tell Kyle who they were seeing. Peter VanHoven had somehow figured out what they were up to and was racing for his battered red truck.

Accelerating as much as he dared without drawing undue attention, Kyle angled the black SUV into a spot in front of a slow-moving gray sedan and joined passing traffic.

He saw the red truck come to life and start down the same crammed exit lane that had delayed their departure. Rachel swiveled in the seat to watch so Kyle made it her assignment. "Let me know how long a line he gets stuck in, okay?"

"Oh, no!" Her gasping reply sent a shiver the length of Kyle's spine.

His hands gripped the wheel, his senses on full alert as he angled to check his mirrors. "What? I can't see him anymore. Where did he go?"

"Over the curb," she shouted. "He's already in the street. Ahead of us!"

FOUR

Rachel couldn't breathe. Every muscle in her body knotted, and she felt trapped in the kind of nightmare where she opened her mouth to scream and no sound emerged. The only thing remotely functional was her brain's ability to call out to her heavenly Father. There were no apt words. Just a silent plea for divine help.

Thankfully, she was braced against the dash with one hand, the other on the back of the seat, when Kyle whipped the steering wheel and accelerated. The SUV bumped up over the right-hand curb with a twist of its chassis. All wheels were spinning when they hit the lawn. Grass churned and clumps flew out behind them.

Horns honked. Bystanders put cell phones to their ears. She finally found her voice. "What are you doing?"

"Getting away."

"You're causing a scene. People are staring at us."

"Doesn't matter," he countered. "Peter already knows where we are or he wouldn't have jumped the line to get ahead."

"But…"

"Just hang on. Is Natalie okay?"

"Yes. She's stirring but still asleep. She must be exhausted."

"No doubt." His next turn was so abrupt the rear of the SUV fishtailed. Straightening out the vehicle and dropping its tires back onto the pavement, Kyle asked, "Do you still see him?"

"No, I…" Her breath caught. "Yes! He's turning off like you did. I hear sirens but they sound far away."

"Could be for some other reason," he said. "Keep watching."

She had no intention of doing anything else. The old red pickup was on their tail all right, but it apparently didn't have four-wheel drive, because it was doing a lot of slipping and sliding while digging curved trenches in the turf. That was an unexpected plus.

"He's losing traction on the grass," she shouted. "We're pulling ahead."

"As soon as he hits the asphalt again he'll have power," Kyle yelled back. "I'm going to head for the highway so we don't cause an accident on these city streets."

"Will we be able to outrun him?"

"Temporarily. But the hospital found you, so he'll be able to, too."

"If it was just the two of us I'd say *stop and have it out with him.*"

"So would I," Kyle agreed. "We can't take a chance with Natalie. Once you—we—took off with her, we stepped across a line. Involving the police at this point won't help us. And it might help Peter."

Rachel was nodding. "Right. If it was only foster care she faced I wouldn't worry too much. We can't trust Peter to leave her alone. He's likely to kidnap her and disappear."

"My thoughts exactly."

Two more sharp turns and they were starting up the

on-ramp to the highway. Rachel spotted a problem. "This is east. We want to go west."

"All I care about is speed and safety," Kyle said flatly. "Keep watching."

"I am, I am." She had swiveled to face forward again so she could peer into the right-hand outside mirror. *Blue car, white car, semi, space, Peter!* She screamed. "He's hiding behind that truck in the far right lane."

"I don't see him."

"Hang on. You will." One of Rachel's hands was fisted around the door handle. The other grasped the edge of her seat. In the mirror's reflection the big truck was falling back. A flash of red swerved out to pass and nearly collided with a second semi. Rachel gasped as that truck driver laid on his horn and barely avoided an accident.

"He's going to get us or somebody else killed," Kyle shouted. "We can't endanger Natalie like this. I'm going to try to lose him."

She refrained from comment because nothing that came to mind lacked sarcasm. They were caught between a rock and a hard place. To stop would put the little girl in ongoing danger and to continue as they were made that threat immediate. Nevertheless, she was glad it was Kyle at the wheel and not her. Defensive driving was not her strongest talent and she was already queasy from riding backward.

"You may want to close your eyes," he yelled as he whipped the wheel at the last instant, cut across two lanes and left Peter trapped on the wrong side of the speeding semis.

Rachel rolled down her window and leaned out, preparing to lose her breakfast, but the gust of cold air shocked the nausea out of her. "You're crazy!"

"I'm successful," Kyle countered with a tight smile.

"He won't have a chance to get off until the next ramp. By that time, we'll have a good head start."

Wind whipped her hair, the tendrils stinging her cheeks. Tears filled her eyes. Had he really done it? Were they safe for the time being? After such a harrowing chase, it seemed impossible.

She sagged against the door, her seat belt holding her. They were passing under the highway, ready to start back in the other direction, when she pushed away and closed the window. "I suppose I should thank you for scaring me to death. Would you mind driving like a normal person from now on?"

Kyle turned briefly to flash a smile. He looked elated as well as short of breath. That was comforting. She'd have been really worried if she'd believed he viewed his stunt driving as everyday behavior.

"Right. Normal. Normal is good," he said. "The speed limit here is high. As long as we maintain our lead we'll be fine."

"Do you think Peter will give up?"

"It's possible. I doubt he had time to listen to the whole story about Angela when he got to ICU. He may go back there."

"Wishful thinking?" Rachel managed a slight smile. "He knows enough. He wouldn't have chased us if he hadn't heard we had Natalie."

"That's probably true."

"And speaking of my niece, I suppose, since this is a civilian matter, I'll need to retain private counsel to defend my right to keep and raise her."

"Uh-huh. I have a couple of connections in San Antonio from my days in the regular world. If you'd like, I can contact them for you."

"I'd appreciate it. Thanks." Realizing she was hoarse,

Rachel was reminded that an apology was called for. "Sorry I yelled at you, Kyle. Guess I got a little too excited."

"We both did." A gentle smile lifted the corners of his mouth and crinkled the outer edges of his dark eyes as he leaned to study the sleepy child in his mirror. "I don't want to stop if we don't have to. Can you make sure she's okay from up here?"

"Sure." Undoing her seat belt, Rachel got onto her knees and leaned over the back of her seat. "Natalie's breathing evenly and is totally relaxed. I guess she's comfortable being with us even if you do drive like you're competing in the Indy 500."

"I'm better than that," Kyle teased. "All they have to do is keep turning left and going around in circles. I not only go both ways, I sometimes jump the car right off the ground."

"Tell me about it." She rolled her eyes, straightened in her seat and clicked her belt back on before touching his forearm. His muscles twitched but he didn't pull away. "I want to thank you. All kidding aside, that was some great driving."

She saw him eye the placement of her hand before he smiled again and said, "My pleasure."

Rachel chuckled quietly. "It was, wasn't it? You enjoyed every minute of it."

"Not totally. If I'd been alone I would have. With passengers it was different."

"*I* trusted you."

She felt the shaking of his arm before she noticed it came from his shoulders. She gritted her teeth. He was silently laughing! At her. And after she had restrained herself from telling him what she'd really thought of his methods. "What's so funny, *Doctor*?"

"You are." Kyle snorted. "For somebody who trusted me, you sure did a lot of screaming."

Clouds had obscured the sun, and wind had begun to gust across the sandy soil as they neared the air base. They were preparing to enter through the south gate when Kyle saw a dot of red closing the distance behind them.

He quickly rolled down his window, flashed his ID at the guard and jerked a thumb behind him. "There may be a guy in a red pickup coming this way. Whatever you do, don't let him through."

"Yes, sir. Shall I call Security?"

"Not unless he gives you trouble. He hasn't actually done anything to us that we can prove and we'd like to keep it that way."

In the background, Rachel gasped. Kyle held his hand out to signal her silence. As soon as they'd left the guard post, she said plenty. "Hasn't done anything? What about my sister?"

"That's a different case. We can assume he's out on bail. If we start bringing up the reason he's chasing us, that will reveal who our passenger is and stir up a hornet's nest. I doubt Peter will say much because he won't want to call attention to his actions, either."

Slowing, Kyle watched the rearview mirrors until he was satisfied the gate guard had repelled their nemesis. "Done. We should be okay for a little while. I'll drop you and your niece at your place and run over to the base exchange for whatever she needs."

"Start with warm clothes." Rachel leaned to peer up at the sky. "Looks like a storm is brewing."

"That, it does." He wheeled expertly into the driveway of her apartment building and parked behind it. "Want me to walk you in?"

It didn't surprise him a bit when Rachel insisted she was capable of managing Natalie and her belongings all by herself. Matter of fact, she had the child out of the SUV and well in hand by the time he circled and stood next to her. "What about sizes? Shall I guess?"

"When in doubt, go big," Rachel told him. "I'll leave the tags on until we see what fits. We can return the rest." Pausing, she smiled. "Thanks for doing this. We really do appreciate everything."

"You're welcome." Kyle thought of adding *My pleasure* again but restrained himself. He didn't want anyone, especially Rachel Fielding, making too much of his efforts. He'd have done the same for any of his techs. It just so happened that this particular airman was beginning to seem special, which was no problem as long as he didn't break regulations and try to date her. The rules against officers and enlisted personnel getting together for romance had never concerned him before.

"And they don't bother me now," he told himself firmly as he drove toward the BX, base exchange, to go shopping for Natalie. There were good reasons for strictness in regard to separation of ranks. Promotions were earned on merit, not based on who an airman knew or who their family happened to be. Every new enlistee was tested and placed according to skills and aptitude. He, for instance, would have made a lousy pilot because of a childhood injury to his inner ear and thus his balance.

Maybe that was why he'd empathized so readily with Rachel and her sister, Kyle reasoned. It had been a long time since he'd thought about the fights his younger brother, Dave, used to get into. And even longer since he'd remembered being injured sticking up for him. Their older sister, Gloria, had already left home by that time and neither of the boys had told their parents about the beatings Kyle had taken defending Dave. Not that it mattered anymore. Gloria was stationed overseas in the army, and Dave had cut all ties after their parents had relocated to Florida. In a way, his family was no closer than Rachel's had been. He'd hoped to change that pattern with Sue and Wendy until their lives had been snatched away so unfairly.

Mad at himself for allowing such maudlin thoughts, Kyle pulled into the parking lot of the base exchange, climbed out and slammed the door. Cold wind hit him in the face. He zipped his jacket and wished he'd thought to bring a hat. To say he was out of sorts was an understatement. This was just the beginning. Now he was going to have to look at children's clothing and that would make him think about how precious his daughter had been.

The mall entrance was festooned with garlands and blinking colored lights. *Christmas.* A season that was supposed to make him feel joyous. Peaceful. Loved.

He clenched his jaw. Love was overrated. So was the holiday. Oh, he respected the spiritual aspects of it: the celebration of the coming of the Savior. It was the *ho-ho-ho* and all the other folderol that he could do without.

Electronic doors slid open. Kyle stomped in. As long as nobody wished him a *Merry Christmas* he could probably get through this task without too much trouble.

He went straight to the children's-clothing section, then paused in front of a display of warm coats. His Wendy had had a red one a lot like this, with a fake-fur collar and white earmuffs to match. No way could he bring himself to buy that same outfit.

Mumbling to himself, he turned away to look elsewhere. His gut was in knots and he was beginning to perspire. Four long years had passed since his family had been wiped out.

It wasn't supposed to hurt this much anymore.

FIVE

Rachel's bravado faded as she surveyed her apartment and considered her new responsibility. What should she do first? What did kids need? "Are you hungry, Natalie? I'm sure I have the makings of a grilled-cheese sandwich."

The shy child nodded.

"Would you rather have something else?"

"Ice cream."

Rachel smiled. "Of course. Silly me. Tell you what. Let me make you something regular to eat and then we'll talk about dessert. Okay?"

Another nod.

"Besides, didn't you have ice cream with Maria and Kyle?"

"Uh-huh." She brightened. "He got me two scoops."

"Wow, that's great."

"Is he coming back?"

"Of course he is."

"Really truly?"

"Honest." Rachel dropped into a crouch and cupped Natalie's thin shoulders. "Oh, you feel chilly. Would you like to wear one of my sweaters?"

"I had a sweater. A pink one. It's ruined."

"I'm sorry, honey," She stood and held out a hand.

"Come on. Let's go look in my room and pick out something you like. It'll be big but warm."

Tears filled the wide blue eyes and Rachel imagined looking into Angela's. "I promise I'll take good care of you, sweetheart."

"I miss Mommy."

Scooping the little girl up, Rachel held her tight and bit back her own sorrow. "I do, too, honey. I do, too."

Natalie's thin arms encircled Rachel's neck. "I'm scared."

"Don't be scared. I'll look after you."

"Peter's mean."

Rachel started to carry Natalie toward the bedroom. "I know. But you're safe here with me. I have lots of friends like Kyle and a whole bunch of wonderful dogs that will protect us both."

"You do?"

"Uh-huh. As soon as Captain Roark—Kyle—gets back, maybe we can go visit the kennels. There's one special dog who's a tripod. I know you'll like him."

"What's a tripod?"

"That means he only has three legs. Stryker is very brave. He was hurt so he got to come home to get better. Kyle is a doctor who fixes injured animals, and he's helping Stryker get well."

"Was he beated like Mommy?"

Rachel pulled the thin body closer to offer more comfort as she said, "No. Not like Mommy. Stryker was in a war a long way away when he got hurt."

The child's voice was thin and reedy when she asked, "Is he gonna die, too?"

"No, baby, no. Stryker is getting better. He's going to be fine. We just have to teach him to walk with a new leg called a prosthesis. But he doesn't have to go back and fight anymore."

"Is he mean?"

"Not at all. You don't have to worry. I won't let you play with any dogs I think are dangerous."

"I wish he was mean," Natalie said. "I'd tell him to go bite Peter real, real hard." With that, she buried her face against Rachel's shoulder.

There was nothing appropriate for rebuttal. Anger was a part of grieving, as was sorrow. Just because Natalie was a five-year-old didn't mean she wouldn't have the same feelings of bereavement that adults suffered. Healing of her wounded spirit would take a while.

For the first time, Rachel realized that she and her niece were probably both suffering from a form of post-traumatic stress. If she understood anything, she understood that. Medical professionals used to refer to it as a disorder, hence the initials *PTSD*. Recently, however, many had begun to see it as more of a syndrome. Semantics aside, she thought it was better to keep from saddling sufferers with a label. Some found post-traumatic stress had to be fought daily. In others, it eventually subsided enough for the patients to carry on normal lives.

Would she ever get over losing her sister? Rachel wondered. Yes, and no. Angela had been a part of her life that she'd never forget. As with the loss of their parents, there would be confusion and undeserved guilt until she was able to accept the inevitable. The same went for Natalie.

Except now they had each other. If that wasn't enough, she'd arrange for counseling. Whatever she had to do, she'd do. There was no maybe about it. She who had despaired of ever having a family had just become an instant mother. And the responsibility scared her witless.

* * *

As Kyle had hoped, he didn't encounter anyone from the K-9 unit before he got the child's clothing to his car. He didn't want to have to explain that he had special permission from Lieutenant General Hall to spend so much off-duty time with an enlisted airman. Besides, the next few days and weeks were going to be critical for Rachel and her niece and they didn't need more trouble. If Peter chose to go to the police and claim abduction, as a normal father would, Rachel could end up in jail and the child sent to foster care despite all their efforts.

Kyle huffed, realizing he was almost glad VanHoven was the kind of person likely to avoid the cops. Except that meant he'd be more apt to act on his own, meaning he'd do whatever it took to get even with Rachel and reclaim his daughter. Kyle could actually identify. He'd have done anything to get Wendy back.

He slammed a fist against the steering wheel. "Stop it. Just stop it. They're gone. Get over it."

That was impossible, of course. During the past four years he had mellowed and stopped experiencing sharp pangs of grief that stopped him in his tracks. But the ache lingered. Being mixed up in Rachel Fielding's dilemma was sure not helping, particularly so near to Christmas.

As he climbed out of the SUV with his purchases, he steeled himself for what he was about to face. A moment's pause was enough for "Father God. Why me? And why now?" Yes, he wanted to be released from the responsibility he felt. And yes, he was ashamed of himself. That didn't keep him from asking.

Sighing, he knocked on Rachel's door. There was no answer. He tried the knob. The door was locked. "Rachel?"

No reply.

Kyle raised his voice. "Rachel! Open up. Let me in."

Still no one called back to him. He dropped the plastic shopping bags, grabbed his cell phone and dialed the private number she'd given him on the way to the hospital.

Instead of the voice on the phone he'd expected, he heard a tentative response through the locked door. "Kyle?"

"Yes. It's me."

"Prove it. What's your rank?"

"Captain. What's going on?"

She threw open the door, grabbed his sleeve and tried to yank him inside before he had a chance to gather up his purchases. Her eyes were so wide they looked surreal. He brought everything in and closed the door. "Why didn't you answer your phone?"

"It's been ringing, but nobody is ever there when I say *hello*."

Kyle heard the ringing again and took the phone from her, not saying anything when he answered. Just as he was about to hang up, a gruff voice said, "You'll be sorry, Rachel," then abruptly broke the connection.

"Was that him? Was it Peter?"

"I assume so, yes."

"What—what did he say?"

"Nothing earth shattering. Just that you'd be sorry."

With a gasp, she was in Kyle's arms before he had a chance to give her back her phone. Not only that—Natalie had grabbed onto his knee and was hanging on as if he were her only lifeline from a sinking ship. "Easy, easy," Kyle said. "Don't panic. He probably got your number from somebody at the hospital."

"No." Speaking with her cheek pressed to his shoulder, Rachel was trembling. "The hospital called the base, not me. Remember? My cell is unlisted. On purpose."

He turned her, encircling her shoulder with one arm after he'd picked up the little girl with the other. "Then he must have gotten it from your sister's old phone. How long has it been since you changed your number?"

"I—I kept it the same so Angie could reach me."

He felt some of the tension leaving her, so he gestured to the sofa. "Sit down and take a deep breath. Empty threats can't hurt you."

"I know Peter, okay? There's nothing *empty* about his threats."

"Okay. I believe you. Now, think. If he'd been able to get on base he would have shown up, not called you. Right?"

"I guess."

"So, he's a nasty piece of work but you're safe here."

"If you say so."

"You don't sound convinced. Tell you what. How about we go get Stryker and see how he does bunking with you? He's been introduced to some of the older children at the base day care and there was no problem, plus you've bonded well. You'll just need to keep an eye on Natalie to make sure she's not too hard on him."

"The doggie Aunt Rachel told me about?" Natalie was almost smiling, something Kyle had not seen her do before.

He crouched in front of the sofa. "That's right. He's kind of big but he's very nice. And he'll bark if anything is wrong so you won't have to be scared when he's being quiet. How does that sound?"

"Maria has a kitty. She scratches."

"Stryker won't scratch you. But you will have to be careful to not bump his shoulder. It's still a little sore."

"He got hurted, huh?"

"He did. But I fixed him."

The child's smile faded. "I wish you could fix my mommy."

Kyle nodded as his heart broke for her. "I wish I could, too, honey. But sometimes, no matter how hard we try, we can't fix everything."

"That's what Maria said when we prayed. I guess God is mad at me."

Rachel spoke up and drew her closer. "No, honey, no. God isn't mad at you. He loves you."

Cuddling against her, Natalie whispered, "I love you, too."

The child's voice was soft, gentle and full of trust. *Just the way Wendy's used to be*, Kyle thought. Children loved without reason or argument. They simply opened up and let it flow.

There was a time when he'd believed his heart had done the same, but those days were over. As a sensible adult he realized that love was far too complex, hard to find and impossible to hang on to. All it did was leave behind painful scars. That was why he'd had no trouble remaining single. No trouble at all.

Sensing that Rachel was staring at him, he stood and turned away. Whatever clues she thought she'd seen on his face were his business, not hers. The sooner he could get in touch with an attorney and set up her defense for taking the child the way she had, the sooner he'd be able to back off and resume their former employer-employee relationship. Yes, he had permission to help her, but he knew he'd be in hot water if the general suspected they were on the verge of becoming romantically involved, as well. Too bad she wasn't also an officer.

That thought struck Kyle a blow that nearly staggered him. If Rachel were an officer, then she and he could date openly. Or more. What in the world was the matter with him? Was he crazy? He hadn't thought about dating anybody in years. Oh, he wasn't brain-dead. He still noticed attractive women. But that didn't mean he made any moves to *court* them.

The difference was the child-mother scenario. It had to be. He was merely equating Rachel and Natalie with the loved ones he'd lost so tragically. Those memories must be coloring his current emotions and throwing off his logic. If he intended to stay in the air force he'd better get a handle on those rampant emotions before he risked his rank and maybe his entire career.

Once in a while there were exceptions made, of course. Even strict rules could be broken with proper permission, such as that which he was currently operating under. It was the possible consequences of carrying things too far that concerned him. And speaking of concerns, there were more immediate ones that needed seeing to.

"I'll leave you two to try on the new clothes," he said flatly, turning to her. "I'll go to the office and do preliminary paperwork on Stryker, then bring him back with me." He started for the door. "Lock everything behind me."

Pausing with his hand on the knob, he added, "And the next time I call you, check the number that comes up on your screen and answer, will you? I almost kicked your door in."

"I don't think I have your cell number," she said, grabbing her phone to page through the contacts file.

He was back to her in three long strides, helped himself to her cell phone and entered his number. "You do now. We'll need to see if we can pull Peter's number off incoming call records when I get back, so don't erase anything."

Rachel stood, her spine straight, her eyes narrowing.

"Look, I appreciate everything you've done for me today but despite the mess I happen to be in, I'm not clueless. I took care of myself just fine until Peter showed up and fooled my sister, and I've gotten plenty of commendations for my work in the air force. Don't sell me short. Okay?"

Despite her anger he found himself wanting to smile. With a curt nod he turned away and said, "That's more like it."

Shocked by Kyle's response, Rachel stared at the closing door for a few moments, then hurried to double lock it. When she started back to Natalie she found the child curled into a fetal position on the sofa. Her little arms were pulled in, her hands poking out of the rolled-up sleeves of the bulky borrowed sweater and shielding her head and face. Clearly, that was her typical reaction to adult dissension.

She flinched as Rachel approached and perched on the edge of the cushions next to her. "You don't have to be scared, honey. I'm not mad at you. Neither is Kyle."

When there was no tangible response Rachel began to gently stroke the thin back through the cable knit. "I'm so sorry, Natalie. I didn't mean to sound upset. I just wanted Kyle to stop babying me."

"He—he's nice," the little girl whispered.

"Yes, he is. And I shouldn't have lost my temper with him. I'm sorry for that, too."

"He'll be mad when he comes back."

"No, he won't. He's not like Peter, I promise. And in a lot of ways, I'm not like your mama, either. She let Peter hurt her. I left when he started to hurt me. We don't have to let anybody hurt us. Ever. We can always tell someone, like you probably told Maria. Right?"

A slight nod.

"See? There are lots of nice, friendly people who will be glad to help you if you ask them."

In the back of her mind, Rachel realized she was preparing Natalie for the possibility of being put in foster care, at least temporarily. The more she pondered her dilemma, the more she realized she had few good options. What she'd done at the hospital had been necessary for personal protection and to safeguard the innocent child. What she would have to face in the future to continue doing the same thing was not going to be nearly that easy.

Trying to distract them both, Rachel began to pull clothing out of the shopping bags Kyle had left. He hadn't forgotten a thing. There were even socks and pajamas included. Soft garments. Cute yet serviceable. For a confirmed bachelor he'd done an exemplary job.

Thinking back, she recalled snippets of conversations about his past that she'd ignored at the time. Now, she began to wonder if he'd once had a family. She knew he was presently single because some of the other techs had broken protocol and flirted with him. When they'd gotten nowhere, one or two had blamed a possible traumatic past for his lack of response. Given all the unmistakable masculine vibes she'd picked up by being near him, she wondered if they might be on the right track. Not that it was any of her business. Still, she was curious.

At the bottom of the last bag, Rachel found a stuffed pink bunny. "Hey, look."

Squealing in delight, Natalie hugged it close. "Is this for me, too?"

"Apparently." Rachel was smiling. "It was with your new clothes. Come on. Let's go in the bathroom and clean you up so we can try these things on."

"Why?"

"Because you need a bath."

"I don't like baths."

Instead of stubbornness, Rachel imagined that she was detecting fear. "You don't?"

"No." Her niece was backing away, clutching the bunny and rubbing her cheek against its pink fur.

"Okay. How about a shower? I can help you wash your hair."

Natalie clapped a hand on the top of her head. "Not my hair. That hurts." Tears gathered in her eyes and she looked unduly frightened. "A lot."

"I'll be very gentle, I promise."

Hand in hand they headed for the small bathroom. The more Rachel learned, the worse her opinion of the child's prior home situation got. No telling how much emotional damage had already been done to this sensitive baby.

Rachel was toweling Natalie dry when her phone rang again. A knee-jerk reaction caused her to jump before making a grab for it. Caller ID showed an unknown number. It wasn't Kyle. Nor was it any of her friends on base. She considered not answering, but this time she had something to say. This time, she was going to tell Peter what she thought of his cruel parenting.

"Finish drying and put on clean clothes while I talk on the phone," she told Natalie.

Once in the hallway she slid the green bar to connect and said, "Listen, Peter," leaving her caller no time to respond before she launched into a tirade. Her hands were trembling but her voice stayed strong until she ran out of steam.

Instead of cringing, Peter laughed. "Are you through? Because I can wait out here all night."

Rachel's breath caught. "What do you mean?"

"Exactly what I said. I can see in your back windows

but you've pulled the blinds in the front. That's not very welcoming, sister-in-law. After all, we are kin."

Racing to her bedroom window, Rachel lowered the shade, nearly dropping the phone as she ended the call. Was he really out there, watching, or had he guessed about her windows? She couldn't take the chance. She had to leave, to keep running. But where could she go? And how? If she left while still a member of the air force it would be considered desertion!

"He wants to make me a fugitive," Rachel muttered. "If I run, he wins. But if I stay here, I'm a sitting duck."

Taking a couple of quick breaths to try to settle her nerves, she pulled up Kyle's number and called him.

"I'm almost there. Is everything all right?" he answered.

"No!" She had to fight to keep from screeching. "Peter called again. He said he's out there. Watching."

SIX

Kyle would have run full out if he hadn't had to slow down for Stryker's sake. "Heel!"

The German shepherd was panting as he half stepped, half hopped along, but was giving no signs of perceiving danger. "That's it, boy. You can do it. Come on."

Raising his fist to knock on Rachel's door, Kyle was taken aback when she jerked the door open. One hand gripped her cell phone, the other, the doorknob. "Hurry. Come in."

He sidestepped for the sake of the dog. Stryker's tail was wagging a mile a minute, his whole rear end taking part in the joyful greeting. As soon as Rachel slammed and locked the door, he was poking his huge black nose at her hand.

Kyle held him in check. "You heard from Peter again?"

"Yes. Did you see anybody lurking outside?"

"No. Neither did this dog. What made you think Peter was here?"

"He phoned and said he was."

"And you answered? Why?"

"Because I wanted to give him a piece of my mind, that's why."

"Are you sure you can spare it?" Kyle was scowling at her.

"Ha ha. Very funny."

"It wasn't supposed to be. This is no laughing matter."

"I know that. And I think he was bluffing. There's no way he could have gotten onto this base so fast. We've only been home an hour or so."

"Then why were you panicky?"

"I don't know. I guess it hit me harder because I was here alone." Kyle watched her expression morph from one of fear and anger to something more rational. "I'm okay, now that Stryker is here with us."

"Good." He smiled over at Natalie. "I see some of those things I picked out were the right size." He held out his hand. "Come here and meet your new buddy."

Although the child was hesitant, she did obey. Stryker, on the other hand, acted as if he'd forgotten all his training, including company manners, the moment Natalie drew near. He strained at the short leash until Kyle had to correct him. "Stryker, back. Sit."

The dog managed to feign a sit without actually putting his rear on the ground. The tail continued to sweep the floor and excitement made him wiggle all over.

Catching Rachel's eye, Kyle made a face. "I've never seen him quite this eager to meet anybody."

"Neither have I. I gather he was raised around kids before we acquired him for the K-9 program."

"That would be my guess."

Kyle crouched next to the shepherd. "Stryker, meet Natalie. Natalie, this is Stryker. He can't shake hands because he needs his front leg to hold himself up, but if you stick out your hand, I know he'd like to sniff your fingers."

She stayed frozen in place so Kyle purposely grinned

at her. "When you're ready, he will be. Here. You can feed him some treats I brought along." To his relief, she slowly extended her hand and accepted the treat.

Stryker, obviously sensing her reluctance, leaned in politely and gave the tips of her fingers a friendly sniff before licking up the tiny morsel.

She pulled back and giggled. "That tickles."

"Would you like to pet him? His fur is really soft, especially his ears. Just be gentle and move slowly. I can see he wants to be your new best friend."

Instead of replying, the little girl reached out and touched the tips of the shepherd's whiskers, then began to stroke the side of his face. He leaned into her hand as if they had been together since he was a pup.

Kyle heard Rachel sigh and felt like echoing that sentiment. This pairing was better than he'd expected. Much better. And, given Peter's continuing harassment, that was more than advantageous. It was an amazing blessing.

In the ensuing minutes, Natalie sat down on the floor and Stryker followed, resting his head on her lap while she continued to pet him. She even ventured to stroke the shoulder above his healing front leg, where short hair had begun to cover the scars, and whisper to him that he was going to be better soon.

It was all Kyle could do to keep from becoming overly emotional. Rachel had already lost that battle and was swiping tears from her cheeks. "Wow."

Kyle cleared his throat. "Yeah. Wow. I don't think we're going to have any trouble acclimating him to staying with you."

"I was already considering filling out the papers to adopt him. Now I know I will."

"You have other more pressing concerns," he reminded her. "Like adopting your niece."

"I know." She eased away from the comfortable pair on the floor and motioned to Kyle to follow. "You can help me sort the clothes you bought. I think most of them are perfect and getting three different sizes of the same shoe was genius."

He looked from her to the child and dog. "I think we should keep an eye on these two for a little longer."

"We need to talk privately."

"In the kitchen, then. I can see them from there and you can make us some coffee." He quirked a smile at her. "Unless you want me to do it. I wouldn't want you to think I was relegating you to the kitchen just because you're a woman."

"Were you?"

He raised his hands in surrender. "Guilty. But this is your home. You know where you keep everything so it does make sense."

"Apology accepted."

He suppressed a smile as he followed her. "What apology?"

The arch of her eyebrows told him he was treading on shaky ground, so he sobered. "Okay. Let's hear it. What did Peter say that had you so spooked?"

"Other than hinting that he was watching me through the windows?" She inclined her head back toward her niece. "She was scared to let me wash her hair because she said it always hurt. Maybe I'm imagining things, but chances are that was no accident. It's just the kind of subtle punishment Peter used to dish out—until he'd finally lose his temper completely and start swinging."

"The poor little thing." Anger surged. Kyle clenched his fists. "That's inexcusable."

"At least we agree on something."

"Oh, I think we agree on lots of things," Kyle said,

"including the fact that VanHoven is the last person who should parent a child. I can see why you were so determined to get her away from him."

"How can we keep her safe?"

"I'm not sure. Even if she went into foster care that's no guarantee he wouldn't continue to pursue her."

"Exactly."

"However, if he reports her as kidnapped, then we're breaking the law." It didn't escape his notice that they were referring to themselves as *we*. As partners in crime. He didn't like the idea but saw no alternative other than turning the little girl over to the authorities.

"I've never even gotten a parking ticket," Rachel said.

Neither had he. If this situation wasn't resolved quickly, though, they were both likely to get more than a simple ticket.

A whole lot more.

Rachel had busied herself making a fresh pot of coffee and figuring out what to serve for supper. Anything but letting herself dwell on the possibilities facing her regarding Natalie. And, by virtue of his assistance, Kyle Roark, too. If she hadn't been so worried about her niece's future she'd have fixated on Kyle's dilemma. Not only was he pushing against the rules of conduct for an airforce officer by siding with her, but he might be risking his whole career. Yes, he could always go back to practicing veterinary medicine in the private sector, but not if he was serving a prison sentence for kidnapping.

"There has to be a solution," she said as she prepared grilled-cheese sandwiches and a salad.

"If you know of one, feel free to share," Kyle replied. "I'm all ears."

"You never should have gotten involved in my problems."

"Tell me about it."

"I just did."

"Yeah, well, you're a little late."

"And I'm sorry about that." She glanced across the kitchen island to check on Natalie for the hundredth time. "You can still walk away. I'll tell the police that you didn't know what you were getting into. It'll be the truth. Neither one of us had a clue what would happen when we started for the hospital in San Antonio."

"That much is true. But we know now."

"That's the biggest drawback. When we were in the throes of panic—or at least I was—and fleeing from Peter, we could be excused if we claimed fear for the welfare of a minor. Now we have a better idea of what my sister and niece went through but no real proof other than what Natalie said. Any further actions we take will have to be fully justified and even then it might not be enough."

Kyle's lips were pressed into a thin line, telegraphing agreement. Finally, he spoke. "I think I should give General Hall another call and fill him in. If he orders the Security Forces to monitor your apartment, that should keep Peter from getting too close to Natalie."

"What if the general won't? Or suppose he tells you to stop helping me? You're not a cop—you're a veterinarian. The top brass may want you to stay completely away from me, for your own safety. Your skills are much more important to the K-9 unit than mine are."

"You are *not* expendable," Kyle insisted.

"In this instance I am."

"Not to me."

In Rachel's eyes he'd instantly attained superhero status. Yes, she realized there was a wide gap between telling her she was worthwhile and expressing affection. However, she had no intention of questioning his motives and taking the chance she had misinterpreted the importance of those three simple words. It was much more comforting to let her imagination take flight like an F-15 and soar above the clouds of doubt blanketing her heart and mind.

Blushing, she told him, "Thank you," and smiled. She might have continued if Stryker hadn't suddenly raised his head, looked toward the front door and growled.

Rachel froze. Natalie acted surprised and a little frightened. Only Kyle reacted defensively. He crossed the short distance to kneel by the dog and heed his warning. "What is it, boy? What did you hear?"

Despite the slippery floor, Stryker was standing by the time Rachel reached her niece. On full alert, he was more than impressive. He was magnificent. No one in his right mind would knowingly challenge a trained K-9 like him—even one with only three legs.

But *was* Peter in his right mind? she asked herself. That was a good question, particularly given all she'd learned since being reunited with her poor sister. His ego had always been puffed up and his temper short. Aging had apparently not brought maturity or better coping skills. On the contrary, he'd grown more cruel, not less.

She picked up Natalie and backed away, holding the child close. How long could they go on like this, jumping at shadows or perhaps facing a flesh-and-blood nemesis? This was only the first day of their hazardous journey toward a new life. How could they possibly give this little waif the peace and security she needed when they were constantly on edge?

Kyle checked the hallway with Stryker and quickly returned to report no signs of a prowler, particularly Peter. "It might help if we had something of VanHoven's to give the dog his scent, but for now, we're safe. I don't know what he heard or smelled to make him go on alert. There was nobody out there."

Pacing while carrying her niece, Rachel tried to decide what her next move should be. She stopped and faced Kyle, eyeing him and the K-9 beside him. "Look. Stryker's a comfort because he'll sense trouble long before I do, but his ability to physically defend against an attack is limited." Kyle opened his mouth, evidently intending to refute her conclusion, so she forged on before he could. "I can't stay here. *We* can't stay here. Natalie and I need to go into hiding."

"That's a pretty drastic choice," he countered. "All the guy has done is phone with veiled threats. First he'd have to sneak onto the base for real, assuming he was bluffing before. Somebody's sure to spot him."

"And do what? If he acted normal they might not even pay attention, let alone report him."

"I'll notify the Security Forces office and make sure word is passed to all the units. Lieutenant General Hall seemed quite sympathetic when I asked him for permission to assist you further. I'm sure he'll be glad to assign official protection, too."

"What if he doesn't?"

She could tell Kyle was wrestling with his reply. The supposition of denial was logical on her part. Peter wasn't a terrorist—unless you counted terrorizing his loved ones—so there was really no valid reason to have her watched or monitored now that she was back home on a secure air base.

Kyle checked the time. "It's not very late. I'll give his office a call and leave a voice-mail message. He wanted me to report once we were back on base anyway and I hadn't gotten around to it. Chances are he'll check his messages before he turns in for the night and might even get back to me."

"What's that old saying?" Rachel asked, "'It's better to ask forgiveness afterward than to ask permission before and be denied'?"

"I haven't read that in the regulations," he quipped cynically. "Don't worry. I'll handle Hall."

Rachel took a deep breath and released it in a noisy sigh. "It's not him, or you, I'm worried about. It's Peter. I know what he's capable of, believe me. You should, too, after what you saw in San Antonio. He won't quit just because my sister is gone."

Rachel lowered her niece to the floor and pointed toward the bathroom. "Why don't you go wash your hands before we eat, honey? Our sandwiches are getting cold and I'm hungry. How about you?"

"Uh-huh. Did you make a sammich for Stryker, too?"

"He has regular dog food that Kyle brought," Rachel reminded her. "Go on. Wash up for me, okay? You can take the dog with you."

"Okay." Her small hand grasped the loop of his short leash and he followed obediently, tail flagging.

As soon as Natalie was out of the room, Rachel approached and stopped close to Kyle. Clearly, he was going to take more convincing than just the word of a child. She was ready. Memory of receiving the injuries she was about to show him made her tremble, yet she must. This was necessary. Not pleasant, but necessary.

He was giving her a quizzical look as she stepped in front of him and began to turn to one side. She hooked a thumb in the neckline of her shirt and pulled it just far enough away from her neck and upper shoulder for him to see the grouping of circular scars. As soon as she heard his sharp intake of breath she released the fabric and faced him.

"That's just the tip of the iceberg. Peter was sadistic when I was a teen, and he still is. Now you won't have to take a child's word for it." Swaying in place, she felt Kyle reach out to steady her.

That was all it took. In moments, she was fully in his arms and leaning on his chest while he whispered against her hair. "He burned you?"

Rachel nodded slightly. Kyle bent and placed a tender kiss on her temple, then began to stroke her back through her shirt. How her arms found their way around his waist was a mystery. She hadn't meant to embrace him, yet there they were, holding each other as if they were far more than comrades in arms. She knew she should pull away. Doubtless, Kyle knew it, too. Still, they remained together as she tried to take in every nuance of the special moment, imprinting it in her brain so she would never lose this amazing feeling of belonging. Was this what real love felt like? Or was she imagining that he returned the fondness she was experiencing?

Kyle's heartbeat echoed hers. Their breathing was in sync. He was resting his chin on the top of her head. Neither made a move to step away until they heard a piercing scream from the direction of the bathroom.

Stryker began to bark.

Kyle was a half second ahead of Rachel running down the hall shouting, "Natalie!"

SEVEN

Rachel paid no mind to anything but the frightened little girl. She pulled Natalie into her arms, held tight and flattened her own spine against the wall to get out of the doorway. The dog whirled and tore out of the bathroom with Kyle in pursuit. Barking continued until they reached her bedroom. Then, it stopped abruptly.

Nothing made a sound—not a peep. She didn't hear boots or Stryker's nails on the hard floor for what seemed like an eternity. Finally, footsteps approached. Kyle was coming back.

"The dog was most interested in your bedroom window," he said. "Since you're on the first floor I assume he heard something. There's nobody out there now."

"If you'd been his partner in a war zone would you doubt him?"

"Probably not. But remember, he's been traumatized. We can't send him to a counselor the way we do people."

Rachel made a derisive noise. "I'd sooner trust any of the K-9s in our unit than most people I know."

"Look, there was nothing there. I don't know what scared Natalie or the dog but it wasn't a prowler."

"And you're sure how?"

"Be sensible, Rachel. I know you've had it rough because of your loss and this new development, but you're acting paranoid."

"I'm only paranoid if nobody is after me."

"The guard stopped Peter at the gate. We saw it happen."

Frustrated, she pushed past Kyle and headed for the kitchen with her niece in her arms. The five-year-old was thin for her age but still felt heavy after a while. Lowering Natalie onto a kitchen chair, she proceeded to take the sandwiches from the warming oven and pass them out. When Kyle followed with Stryker, the dog went straight to the child.

A plan was taking shape in Rachel's mind. Because Kyle didn't believe her, she was going to have to play it safe and leave without his knowledge. Then, when he was questioned, he'd be able to truthfully say he had no idea where she'd taken her niece. Destination was the problem. She had no family left and didn't dare use credit cards or the authorities could trace her whereabouts. How far could she hope to get without her own car and with little cash in her purse? Probably not even out of state. Then again, perhaps this was the Lord's way of forcing her to trust more and stay where she was.

That notion did not sit well. Rachel was used to calling the shots and making her own decisions. If the call about her sister had not come as such a shock, she would have traveled to the hospital alone, which, in retrospect, was exactly what she should have done.

As she sat at the kitchen table and picked at her almost-cold sandwich, she sensed that Kyle was studying her. Finally, he spoke. "Okay. What do you want to do?"

"Go back to yesterday and change it," she said flatly. "But since that's impossible, I guess I'm stuck."

"With me?"

She could tell his feelings were hurt, but because she cared what happened to him, she decided that was better than becoming an accomplice to a crime. The longer he stayed with her, the more he'd look guilty when their reckoning came. "You should go. We'll be fine as long as you leave Stryker with us."

"I see." He rose from the table and threw down his napkin.

Noticing that Natalie was wide eyed and cringing, Rachel quickly defused the situation. She inclined her head toward the child and paused long enough for Kyle to get the message. "I'm glad you're not upset," she said cautiously. "We don't want you to be mad."

"I'm not mad at anybody but myself," he countered. "I just thought…"

Empathetic, Rachel watched him slowly circle the table and bend low to place a kiss on the top of the child's head. "You take good care of Stryker for me, okay? I left a bag of his food on the counter. Make sure he always has water to drink. I'll come back to check on him in the morning."

"Okay."

Then, he focused on Rachel. "I'm still going to ask for a Security Forces watch on this apartment whether you approve or not. If the general doesn't see things my way, I'll make other arrangements. I'm not leaving you unguarded. Understand?"

How could she argue with such a sensible plan? "I do. Thank you for everything."

The obvious pain in his expression was nearly her undoing. There had to be a poignant story behind his emotional response, one she felt compelled to uncover. Following him to the door, she stopped him. "What happened to you in the past, Kyle?"

"I don't know what you're talking about."

"Yes, you do. Tell me. Why is my niece's safety so important to you? Why are you so upset about leaving us?"

"It's the holiday season," he said flatly. "Christmas is always hard for me. Being around you and Natalie at this time of year brought back some strong memories."

"You had a family?" It was a logical guess.

"Once. Long ago. They were killed in a traffic accident on their way home from Christmas shopping."

She laid a hand of consolation on his forearm. "I'm so, so sorry. I didn't know."

"Nobody on base does. It's buried in my file. I never bring it up." His expression hardened. "I'd appreciate it if you kept the information to yourself, as well."

"Of course."

Rachel's heart was breaking for him. She'd caught the poor man at a sensitive moment, and he'd revealed facts he'd been keeping secret. No wonder he was so solicitous to her and Natalie. He was envisioning a second chance, a surrogate family to look after. And the surges of affection she'd detected? Those did not belong to her, but to a woman he had once loved.

Well, so be it. That made her upcoming actions easier. As soon as she could arrange bereavement leave, line up transportation, withdraw some cash from an ATM and buy an untraceable cell phone, she and Natalie would go into hiding. From there she could contact civilian authorities about gaining legal protection, yet keep Peter from knowing where she was. There would be a thin, thin line between what she was doing and what the law dictated, but she'd weather the storm somehow. She had to. A child's welfare depended upon it. And maybe her own survival did, too.

* * *

Kyle had little success convincing his commanding officer that extra patrols were necessary for Rachel's sake. He did, however, speak to Westley James, Linc Colson and a few other CAFB K-9 cops and get them to agree to swing by her apartment more often. That helped ease his mind, but not enough to keep him from spending the night parked outside her building, huddled in his warmest jacket while watching for prowlers.

By first light he was exhausted. A shave and a change of clothes were in order, yet he hated to leave his post. Nothing unusual had occurred. The base had been quiet all night except for occasional takeoffs and landings.

He made a fist and wiped condensation from inside the windshield as a vehicle approached. It was Linc Colson. He stopped parallel to Kyle and rolled down his window.

"Morning. I thought I might find you here, Doc. Brought you some coffee."

"Thanks. I can use it. I was about to head back to my quarters and get into uniform."

"You're not on leave?"

Kyle shook his head as he took a tentative sip. Steam was rising through the hole in the lid. "Um, hot. No, not exactly. Hall said I could leave the base to assist Rachel Fielding yesterday and that problem isn't solved yet."

"What's going on?"

"Possible stalking."

"You must think so, or you wouldn't have slept in your car."

"I didn't want to take any chances."

"Okay. Tell you what. I can hang around here for half an hour or so while you go clean up."

Kyle smiled as he drew his fingers down his cheeks

to meet his thumb at the point of his chin. "I could use a shave. You're sure you don't mind?"

"It's on my patrol route. Now get going so you'll be back before I have to move on."

"Okay. Thanks."

With one last look at the area surrounding the apartment building, Kyle pulled away. He felt like a fool for worrying so much. After all, CAFB was a secure installation. The chances of a lowlife like VanHoven actually finding a way in were slim. So what had held him there all night, watching, guarding?

He thought back to the night when complacency had cost him his family. Light snow had fallen and he'd warned Sue to drive carefully while he'd finished up at his veterinary hospital in Fort Worth. She and Wendy had planned their outing, claiming they were buying special gifts for him. Something had told him he should have gone along, but he'd ignored the feeling in favor of work. Shortly thereafter he'd gotten the news that a drunk driver had wiped out his loved ones.

Kyle's hands were fisted so tightly on the steering wheel his fingers cramped. He'd never been much of a worrier until he'd lost his family. After that, his practice had floundered almost to the point of bankruptcy, leading him to sell out and return to the air force, where he'd finally found peace.

And now? Now he was beginning to feel almost as anxious as he had four years ago. Only it wasn't just plain concern, was it? He cared too much about Rachel as well as her niece. The comparison to his former family had thrown him for a loop to begin with, but he was beginning to envision more from the experience. He was getting too attached. And despite all the obstacles, he couldn't talk himself out of it.

That was almost as unnerving as admitting his burgeoning feelings in the first place.

Rachel got herself and Natalie dressed, fed and ready to go out. It was comforting to note that one of the Security Force SUVs was idling in the street. As long as Rachel's movements were covered and she had the dog, she felt pretty safe.

"Put your new jacket on, honey. Want me to help you zip it?" she asked.

"I can do it."

"Okay. Come on." She tucked her wallet in a coat pocket. "We need to go shopping and this is a perfect time to leave because there's a base police car right out front."

"Where's Kyle? He said he was coming back."

"Not this early."

"Can Stryker go, too?"

"Only as far as the lawn. We'll exercise him while we wait for a cab, then put him back inside."

"Awww."

"It isn't fair to ask him to walk to the store on three legs, and he can't ride in a cab with us because he doesn't have his official vest and badge," Rachel explained.

"He's gonna be lonesome."

"We'll bring him a treat."

"Ice cream?"

Despite being nervous, Rachel had to laugh. "I had something a little more beefy in mind. Maybe a bone?"

"Yuck."

Continuing to chuckle, Rachel took her niece by the hand, the dog's leash in the other. She'd had enough experience with Stryker to know he'd be well behaved as well as protective. Nevertheless, she wasn't confident enough to turn him loose. She hadn't tested him off lead or around distractions like passing traffic and didn't want to endanger him.

They stepped outside. Rays of sunshine had topped the ridge to the east and were blanketing the base with warmth. Although the overall temperature remained low, the sun felt good on her face. Stryker raised his head, ears perked up, tail flagging happily. Keeping one eye on the black patrol vehicle, Rachel gave the shepherd his head and let him sniff all he wanted. Nose to the ground, he led her and Natalie around the side of the building.

She immediately realized where he was focusing. The dry earth beneath her bedroom window was packed too hard to show footprints, but the dog was certainly interested in something there.

Hair at the nape of her neck prickled like the ruff on an angry animal. She pressed her back to the wall and faced out to scan the neighborhood. A board fence delineated the edge of the property. It was high enough to hide a man. Had it? Was that what the K-9 had been trying to tell her?

Freezing for an instant, she considered the possibility her enemy might have lingered nearby. Reason reminded her that Stryker would be barking if that were the case. No. Whoever had been prowling around the night before and had frightened Natalie was long gone. Her fondest hope was that the dog now had a good idea what he smelled like. If it had been Peter, as she feared, that was even better. All Stryker had to do was remember the scent and react if he ever encountered it again.

As soon as Stryker was safely back in the apartment, Natalie tugged on Rachel's hand. "Carry me?"

Rachel opened her arms and lifted her niece, balancing her weight on one hip. "Okay, I'll carry you to the cab. You have to walk when we get to the store, though."

"Okay." Natalie's arms encircled Rachel's neck and she gave her a squeeze. "You're nice."

"Thank you. I try."

"I'm being good, huh?"

"Of course you are. Why?"

The child tucked her head against Rachel's shoulder, hiding her face when she said, "'Cause I don't want you to give me back to Peter." A shudder punctuated the statement.

"I won't. I already promised." Should she explain further? There might not be a better time. "Sometimes children have to stay in other places for a little while until a judge decides where they should go to live. If that happens to us, that doesn't mean you're bad. It's just how the rules work."

"No!"

Rachel patted her back to try to soothe her. "I promise I'll do the best I can to keep you with me, honey. But I can't break the law and be bad like some people are. The only reason I brought you home with me is because I wanted to keep you safe."

"From Peter?"

"Yes. From Peter." She held her tightly. "I want you to tell me if you see him or any of his friends from your old house, okay?"

"Okay."

The taxi crossed Canyon Boulevard. Rachel remained wary as they arrived at their destination. She took the little girl's hand. "Brrr. Let's go in the mall where it's warmer and look around until the bank opens."

The obedient child let Rachel lead her without a fuss. Perhaps it hadn't been wise to tell her about the legal obstacles she expected to face, but it would have been worse to be separated forcibly without Natalie knowing what was happening or why.

The more Rachel mulled over her predicament, the more foolish it seemed to let fear govern her choices. Kyle was right about the security of the base. And while they were there, they had Stryker on their side, too. It was too bad she couldn't take him with her when she fled or she'd be in even worse trouble than she already was.

Weighed down by reality and the supposition that her situation was getting worse by the minute, she plopped down on a bench inside the mall. Unshed tears filled her eyes. She blinked them back. This situation was untenable. They were doomed and it was all her fault, although in retrospect she didn't see how she could have changed the outcome while still protecting the innocent child.

Natalie crawled up beside her and ducked under Rachel's arm, then took hold of her hand with both of her smaller ones. "Don't be sad, Auntie Rachel."

"I'm sorry, baby. I don't mean to be."

"I miss Mommy, too."

Rachel tucked her closer. "I know you do. I'm sorry I'm not more fun. I just don't know what to do right now to fix everything and I wish I did."

She waited for a reply. When it didn't come, she looked down and saw Natalie's head buried against her coat. Slowly, gently, Rachel lifted Natalie's tearstained face and looked into her Fielding blue eyes, expecting mourning. Instead, she saw raw fear.

Without a word, the child lifted her arm and pointed across the polished stone floor. It took Rachel the space of a heartbeat to realize what she was trying to show. Barely thirty feet away stood a man with his back to them. Instead of wearing camo like most of the others nearby, he was dressed in a red satin bomber jacket with worn elbows, jeans and dirty running shoes. *Peter!*

Rachel gasped, grabbed Natalie and swung her around as she ran for the nearest shop entrance. Inside, she bypassed racks of clothing and headed for the dressing rooms. There had to be a back door. There just had to be.

Natalie was sobbing and attracting too much attention. A clerk eyed them suspiciously. "Can I help you?"

"She's just upset because she wants ice cream," Rachel said, grasping at the first excuse that came to mind. "We'll go out the back so we don't disturb your other customers."

"Sorry. We keep that locked. You understand."

"Sure, sure." Clutching the little girl close, Rachel ducked into an empty dressing room and pulled out her cell phone. There was only one person she trusted enough to summon.

"Hush," she told her niece with a finger to her lips. "You need to be really quiet, sweetie. I'm calling Kyle."

EIGHT

Kyle had decided to check on Stryker, then report to the training center. Traffic was heavy on Canyon Boulevard and around the BX. Many airmen had put in for holiday leave, while others were stocking up to celebrate locally. As far as Kyle was concerned, they were all overdoing it. The last time he'd arranged a special Christmas getaway his plans had died with his loved ones. That remembrance usually brought a tightness in his chest and a lump to his throat. This time, however, his reaction was tempered. Softer. More filled with melancholy acceptance than ever before.

As he drove, Kyle heard his cell phone ringing. "Roark."

Someone was panting, muttering unintelligibly.

"Hello? Who is this?"

"Rachel" he was able to make out. Beyond that, her attempts at conversation were muddled.

"Whoa. I can't understand a word you're saying. Slow down and speak up."

"I can't talk louder. We have to be very quiet."

"Where's Sergeant Colson? He's supposed to be right outside your apartment."

"There was a patrol car there. But I'm not home now. I'm at the BX with Natalie."

Inappropriate responses filled his mind. "Where, exactly?"

"I don't know. Some clothing store. It's near the bank."

He thought he heard her mumble again before she blurted, "It's him. We both saw him. Peter is here."

"Why didn't you say so in the first place?" Kyle whipped the wheel and made a U-turn at the next corner. "Stay put. I'm coming."

Weaving between slower cars, he did his best to rush. The harder he tried, the more obstacles appeared. Frustration built. If he went charging into the base exchange mall he'd attract all sorts of attention. Assuming Rachel and Natalie really had spotted Peter, he knew he had to appear as inconspicuous as possible. That, and locate them before the other man did.

Since he had never gotten a close look at VanHoven it was liable to be difficult to pick him out in a crowd, particularly if he'd assumed a disguise and was dressed in the camo ABU, air-force battle uniform, that most airmen wore.

Kyle slid the last corner on two wheels, cut off another car and slipped into an empty parking place. He was out of the SUV and running toward the main entrance in seconds. A few feet from the automatic doors, he slowed and transformed himself into a normal, casual shopper.

The interior of the mall was crowded, good for hiding but bad for spotting an enemy. As his gaze swept the passing throng, he fixated on one anomaly. The clothing matched what he'd seen at the hospital. And the haircut was far from acceptable for any service member. That had to be Peter.

Kyle faded into the shadow of a doorway and watched. More than nervous, Peter appeared to be under the influence of cither drugs or alcohol, maybe both. His mannerisms were jerky and unnatural. He didn't stagger as much as walk with a slight limp.

Edging closer, Kyle got a better look. There was blood on one of the man's ankles and the sleeve of his jacket was torn. Given his grubby condition, it was possible he'd found his way onto the base via one of the washed-out places that occasionally appeared beneath the perimeter fences. If VanHoven had come straight through the woods to the housing area, he might have been able to locate Rachel's apartment, particularly if he'd had help.

At this point, it doesn't matter if he was the prowler Stryker sensed last night or not, Kyle told himself. What he needed to do now was locate Rachel and the child and spirit them away before Peter noticed. Reporting him was out of the question. If VanHoven started screaming for his *daughter*, there would be too much explaining to do. No. First, he needed to rescue Rachel and Natalie. By the time Security picked up Peter, they could be off the base.

Kyle strode past one of the banks that maintained an office in the mall. The next shop featured shoes. After that came one that sold women's clothing.

Taking one last quick peek at Peter, he entered the shop and immediately felt out of place. Why couldn't Rachel have ducked into a sporting-goods store? Pretending to scan the racks of clothes, he worked his way to the rear where the dressing rooms were. Entering was out of the question. So was shouting her name and drawing attention.

"Can I help you, Captain?"

He smiled politely. "I hope so. My wife asked me to meet her down here and she forgot to say which store. I wondered if she might be trying on something."

"Was she alone?" the clerk asked.

"Um, no. Our little girl was with her." He held out a hand, palm down. "About this tall, blond hair, blue eyes."

"Good lungs?" the clerk added with an arch of her brows. "Never mind. I think your wife is here. I'll go get her."

Kyle heard the woman call, "Ma'am, your husband is looking for you. Will you please come out now?"

When Rachel didn't appear he took a chance, leaned in and called, "Hey! Rachel. Are you ready to go?"

She not only came out, she barreled into Kyle's chest and clung to him. Natalie grabbed his knee. "We were afraid it wasn't you."

Instead of asking questions and waiting for her explanation, he lifted Natalie, kept one arm around Rachel's shoulders and started for the door. "Put up the hood on your jacket," he told the child. "We're getting out of here."

All three paused at the store's doorway. Clear glass windows and door gave them no place to hide.

"So far, so good," Kyle said hoarsely. "What were you doing out and about without a bodyguard?"

"I didn't think I'd be allowed to bring Stryker."

"Since when did rules stop you?" he asked cynically.

"I was thinking of the dog, okay? Without his prosthesis it would be harder for him to walk very far."

"What was wrong with staying home?" If he hadn't been looking at her when he'd asked, he might have missed the guilt briefly reflected in her expression. Astonished, he stared. "You were running away from me!"

"What if I was?" Rachel leaned past him to check passersby. "You kept insisting Peter couldn't possibly get on base and he did. What should I have done? Sit at home and wait until he knocked on my door?"

Kyle turned right and headed into the depths of the immense mall, keeping Rachel and Natalie close as he took long, purposeful strides. He had no pat answer for her. Nothing was working out the way he'd imagined. Nevertheless, he did have a few observations.

"First of all," he said with an undertone of anger, "you had no idea that man was actually on the base. Not until you spotted him this morning. So any plans to take off like a fugitive were made before you got here."

She didn't reply. Kyle went on. "Second, if you had intended to tell me what you were up to, you would have phoned before you left your apartment instead of waiting until you were scared to death."

Sensing danger he picked up the pace, making her half jog to keep up. "Third, you'd better hope we can get out of here before Peter spots us and gives chase, because anybody who stops him is going to want to know why he's here and that will point directly to you. And me."

"And Natalie," Rachel finally said.

"Yes. And Natalie. Which is the worst of all three."

"We have to run away. Can't you see that?"

"I'm waiting to hear back from a buddy of mine who's a civilian lawyer. He can probably advise you."

"And in the meantime?"

Kyle could tell she was getting short of breath. Between that and her fear, he wasn't sure how much longer she'd be able to keep up with him. He knew what he should do: call the cops and wait for them to arrive. He also know there were other options, possibilities he'd entertained, then rejected out of hand. He had a place to take her, to hide her, but hadn't been back there in years. Nor was he eager to revisit that part of his past. Why hadn't he sold the tiny cabin long ago? Keeping it up was a useless drain on his finances.

So, why had he hung on to it? *Because it was once a happy place*, Kyle thought with a sigh. A place where his little family had shared holidays and made beautiful memories. Located on an unmarked, forested tract of land, it was so secluded he'd had to convince his late wife, Sue, it was safe to proceed beyond what her GPS could pinpoint.

"My car is parked directly across from the front entrance," Kyle rasped, leaning to speak to Rachel. He pressed a key into her trembling hand. "When we get to the side door, you take Natalie on ahead, get in the SUV and start it. Keep your heads down. I'll be there as soon as I make sure we're not being followed."

Her eyes were wide with fright and glassy with tears. She took a shuddering breath. "Did—did Peter see us?"

"Possibly. I noticed someone moving fast through the crowd. I can't imagine who else it would be."

Panting, Rachel peered past him. "I don't see him."

"That doesn't mean he isn't there."

Wide exit doors slid open. Cold wind rushed in. Kyle set Natalie at Rachel's feet. "Go. Now."

She grabbed her niece's hand, stood on tiptoe and planted a kiss on his cheek. Her lips were warm, her touch gentle yet urgent. Then, without a word, she turned and began to hurry away.

Kyle stared after her. If he'd had any doubt whether to take her to the cabin, that kiss had solidified his decision. He was in this up to his neck and wasn't going to back off.

He stepped aside, stood next to the closing door and waited. If anybody tried to follow Rachel and Natalie, they'd have to take him out first.

Pain sliced through Rachel's lungs and almost doubled her over. She pressed her ribs, hoping that would help. It didn't. She was near the end of her endurance.

Intense fright had sapped her strength as much as physical exertion.

Not sure which vehicle was Kyle's, she pushed the button on Kyle's smart key. Flashing yellow lights led her straight to the SUV. She strapped Natalie in the second seat, as before, and climbed behind the wheel.

Shorter than Kyle, she had to scoot forward on the driver's seat to reach the brake and gas pedals. The engine roared to life. Her hands fisted on the wheel. So far, she'd followed Kyle's orders. *This* was where she intended to deviate. Prayers for transportation off the base had been answered. No one in his right mind would expect her to just curl up on the seat and sit there like the derelict machinery their fighter pilots used for target practice.

Oh, no. She had wheels. She was going to spin them and "get out of Dodge."

One glance back at Natalie assured her that the child was all right. A second glimpse of the sidewalk outside the door showed Kyle standing alone, apparently braced for attack. This was her chance to escape. So why was her conscience screaming at her to not leave him?

"Please, God," Rachel whispered. "Tell me this is okay."

Partially backing out of the parking space, she was delayed by a passing car. There were blind spots in the SUV mirrors that kept her from being certain the other car was far enough away to allow safe egress, so she inched backward.

By the time she had room to straighten the wheels she was perspiring. Natalie must have sensed her anxiety because her thin voice piped up. "Auntie Rachel? Where's Kyle?"

Where, indeed? She looked back at the place where she'd last seen him. Her breath caught; her pulse leaped.

Kyle was down in a blur of male bodies! So was Peter. A couple of airmen had stopped to cheer on the combatants. Nobody seemed inclined to stop the fight. In fact, a third person, in civilian clothes, had just jerked Kyle and Peter to their feet.

For an instant she thought the new arrival was on their side. Then the burly man threw a punch that sent Kyle reeling. That was enough to inspire several airmen to jump into the fray. Fists flew. Men wheeled and staggered, then lunged back into the fight. Where was Kyle? Which one was he? What if they *all* ganged up on him?

Rachel whipped the steering wheel left and floored the gas. Now her decision was easy. She was going to rescue the only real friend she had in the world.

Unarmed, Kyle had made the mistake of assuming Peter was, too. A flash of silver proved otherwise. Kyle knocked the knife aside and closed in, gaining temporary advantage. He barely noticed the gathering spectators— or the wound in his side.

Wiry VanHoven slipped out of his grasp three times before Kyle was able to pin him down. The smaller man fought like a wild animal, or somebody on drugs. Kyle guessed the latter. Superhuman strength was a side effect of meth while it made users unpredictable and irrational. Not the best kind of adversary to face in hand-to-hand combat.

Someone from the crowd wrenched them apart. Fists were flying. He figured the airmen had noticed his captain's insignias and sided with him. That other civilian, however, packed a punch like a mule's kick.

Kyle went down. His jaw ached; his vision blurred. He shook it off and clambered to his feet. Someone slammed him against the outer wall of the building, barely missing the glassed front. In his peripheral vision he glimpsed Peter's jacket. Was he fleeing?

Kyle ducked just in time to avoid another jarring punch from the larger man. Airmen came to his aid and piled on top of the remaining attacker.

Peter was getting away! Kyle yearned to run after him but his image wavered like a desert mirage on a hot Texas afternoon. He staggered. Pressed a hand to his side. Stepped off the curb into the street.

A horn honked. Dizzy, he managed to turn without falling. It was his car! Pulling up right next to him. And Rachel was driving.

The electric window on the passenger side slid smoothly down. She was yelling something but it was drowned out by the noise of the ongoing fight. He reached for the door handle and used it for balance.

"Get in!" she yelled.

Under the circumstances Kyle figured that was a pretty good idea. He pulled himself into place as best he could as she hit the gas. Rapid acceleration threw him back against the seat. He tried to gather his thoughts. Pointed behind them. "Peter is running. He's getting away."

Instead of racing in pursuit as he thought she would, she said, "So are we," and left the parking lot by the farthest opposite exit.

NINE

Rachel's greatest concern was the condition of her companion. "Are you okay? Do we need to go to the hospital?"

Kyle shook his head in what looked like both a reply and an effort to clear his thoughts. "I'm a doctor. I'll take care of myself."

"Not if you pass out. You aren't usually that pale. What's wrong?"

"I'll be fine. Just keep driving."

"Where to?"

"Drive while I think. We can't go back until the cops get their hands on Peter and whoever that man-mountain was he brought with him."

"I thought I saw two guys attacking you but everything happened so fast I wasn't sure."

Kyle winced. "I'm sure. Swing by your place and pick up Stryker. We can't abandon him. Then head for the east gate."

"We're leaving the base after all?"

"Temporarily. I have some calls to make as soon as we're in the clear."

"Who are you going to call?" After what had just happened she trusted him to do the right thing, but that didn't mean she'd stopped worrying.

"Security, first, so they'll know what the fight was about and won't blame the airmen who jumped in to help me. I'm also going to tell them what VanHoven was wearing and warn them that he has a knife."

She caught a glimpse of him peering down at his side. There was blood on his hand! "You're hurt."

"It's not deep. Keep going."

"To the hospital, you mean." They were approaching her apartment building. "I can turn around here."

"No!"

"You don't have to yell. I can probably stitch you up but I'll have a hard time explaining myself if you aren't conscious."

"I doubt sutures will be required," Kyle told her. Although his jaw was clenching when she pulled to the curb, he sounded convincing. "I'll stay with Natalie while you get the dog."

"We could call somebody else to pick him up."

"We could, but I want him with us. We're liable to need all the help we can get."

"Right. But what if Peter shows up before I get back?"

"Trust the K-9," Kyle said. "You know the commands as well as I do. He'll take out Peter if he needs to." She saw him grimace. "Even with three legs he's more threatening than I am like this."

"Okay." Leaving the motor running, she threw open the driver's door and took off toward her apartment. *Please, God*, she prayed, *let Kyle be all right.* The rest of her prayer was jumbled and confusing, yet she knew it included thoughts of love and devotion and the desire to somehow hold her impromptu family together. The fact that such wishes made little sense didn't bother her nearly as much as the possibility they might be pulled apart by circumstances beyond anyone's control.

"Father, help us," she whispered, meaning every word. "We can't do this alone."

When Stryker met her at the door, panting, tail wagging, eager to please, Rachel realized that part of her urgent prayer had been answered before she'd even asked. They already had capable help, ready and willing. Now all they had to do was get off the base and disappear.

Kyle was doing his best to keep his pain at bay. The only sign of suffering he could not control was the perspiration dotting his forehead. "Act calm when we're passing through the gate," he reminded Rachel.

"I wish you'd quit telling me to do that. This may be normal for a guy who's been in combat but it isn't to me."

"Then fake it," he said with a forced chuckle. "I'm glad you decided to do things your own way this time and came to pick me up. I was getting the worst of that fight."

"Probably because you were the only one bleeding," she said, grimacing and eyeing him.

He slipped his hand into the pocket of his jacket and began to apply pressure unobtrusively to hide his injury. With a wave at the nearest guard, they sailed through the gate unchallenged.

Rachel was shaking visibly when she eased her grip on the wheel and reached down to adjust the driver's seat to her size.

"I wondered if you always drove perched on the edge and clinging to the steering wheel."

"I was in a hurry to rescue you," she said with a touch of cynicism.

"Yeah. Thanks."

Kyle phoned a friend at the training unit. "That's right. I was attacked outside the BX. The airmen who came to my aid did *not* instigate the fight." He paused, listening, then said, "When I explained everything to Lieutenant General Hall, he gave me permission to do whatever was necessary to assist one of my techs. As I said before, trouble followed us back from San Antonio. At least two male civilians. Peter VanHoven and an unnamed assailant jumped me. I have no idea how they got on base, but there was dirt on VanHoven's clothing. Security should check perimeter fences. If there are any questions, I'll be available by cell."

When Kyle ended the call he relaxed back against the seat and briefly closed his eyes.

"Are you feeling faint?"

"No. Why?"

"You shut your eyes."

"If you must know, I was praying about our next move."

He checked his phone again. "GPS puts us seventeen miles from my cabin. That's where we're going."

"Your what?"

"Cabin. And don't give me any flack."

"What makes you think that will be any safer than holing up on base?"

"I owned the place before I reenlisted, and I haven't visited there in years."

"Really? Why didn't you sell it?"

"It's a long story," Kyle said. The cabin held poignant memories for him, memories he didn't want to let go of, yet didn't want to be reminded of, either.

He glanced into the side mirror. A passenger car was keeping pace with them despite their speed. Had his decision to pick up Stryker given Peter a chance to track them down? It didn't look good.

* * *

Rachel noticed Kyle's concern before he had time to tell her anything. "Are we being followed?"

"I'm not sure. Get ready to turn off the highway."

"Where?"

"It's coming up." He pointed ahead. "There. Don't slow down on the dirt road."

She complied, surprised at how rough the track was. "This bouncing must be hurting you."

"I'll live. Faster!"

She failed to see anyone behind them due to the brownish cloud they were raising. "They'll see our dust!"

"Can't be helped. Turn off at that pine with a gouge in its trunk. The cabin is just ahead on the right."

"I see it."

"Try to pull behind and get out of sight."

"Wow. It's sure overgrown."

Tense and perspiring, Rachel plowed through the undergrowth, hearing it snap, crush and scrape the sides of the SUV. Their stop was jarring. For a moment she just sat there, catching her breath.

The tiny cabin was pioneer log construction. Casement windows flanked a front door. There was no entrance in the rear. Kyle got out and led the way to a hidden key while Rachel fetched Natalie. Stryker followed.

When Kyle swung open the door the little girl gasped. The interior was a wonderland. Garlands were festooned from the ceiling. Tinsel hung from strings of tiny colored lights. Bright glass orbs twisted on invisible threads.

And in the far corner stood a miniature plastic evergreen tree with a manger scene at its base.

Christmas had been waiting for him for four long years.

TEN

Rachel didn't know what to say. Natalie was clapping her hands and jumping up and down. "Look, Auntie Rachel. Isn't it beautiful?"

"Yes." It was. Truly. Natalie made a dash for the crèche while Kyle checked the windows and reported no one else coming up the road.

"This is baby Jesus," the little girl said. "And these are the wise men. They brought birthday presents. Gold, common sense and fur."

Relieved to have escaped, Rachel smiled at Kyle. "Leave it to kids to put life in perspective. Did you learn about the wise men in Sunday school, honey?"

"Uh-uh. Maria told me. I miss her."

"We can go visit her after I adopt you."

"You're gonna be my mommy?"

"Yes."

The little girl giggled. "That's silly. Then you'd be Auntie Mommy." She paused. "Will Kyle be my new daddy? Please?"

He crouched next to the five-year-old. "I'll always be your friend," he said tenderly. "Your aunt works for me so I'm sure you and I will see each other a lot."

Joining them, Rachel added, "That's right. But there's

a rule in the air force that I'm not supposed to date my boss, so Kyle can't be your daddy."

It took a few seconds for Natalie to process that information. When she had, she was totally candid. "Well, *that's* a dumb rule."

He ruffled her hair. "I agree completely. That is one very dumb rule."

"Maria says we have to be good and keep rules," Natalie told him. "Do we? Even if they're dumb?"

"I'll have to give that question some thought," Kyle told her. "Now you play over here while your aunt Rachel puts a bandage on my owie, okay?"

"Okay."

Rachel followed him to a section of the single room where he'd stored first-aid supplies.

"Use rubbing alcohol to clean the cut." He was taking off his jacket.

More aspects of their isolation began to occur to her. "There's no water?"

"We have fruit juice in cans and enough to eat for a few days. I'll phone the base and let Security know where we are after you patch me up. We'll go back as soon as they have your buddy Peter in custody."

"Do you think he was in the car that followed us?"

"Possibly. But we lost them."

Rachel's hands were trembling as she cleansed the wound. "I think a few butterfly bandages will take care of it."

"You just don't want to suture me."

"It's not something I've always dreamed of doing, no."

"What are your dreams, Rachel? Will they change now that you're about to become Auntie Mommy?"

That made her smile. "There was a time, long ago,

when I wanted a family. Seeing what happened to my sister turned that dream into a nightmare but…"

Kyle touched her hand. Stilled it. Looked into her eyes as if he was able to see all the way to her heart's desires. "But?"

"Our time together has been extraordinary. It's hard to put into words without sounding sappy, but I've looked forward to almost every moment." She lowered her gaze to where his hand touched hers. "Especially to spending more time with you."

"I feel the same." He leaned closer. Rachel felt her cheeks flaming. She closed her eyes, hardly able to believe what she knew was about to happen. His nearness was palpable. A tender touch against her cheek, the whisper of his breath mingling with hers.

And then he kissed her.

Rachel was floating on clouds of intense emotion, yearning for the moment to continue. Kyle's kiss was everything she had hoped, and more. Walls that had stood between them crumbled to dust. Problems that had seemed insurmountable shrank into nothingness. Surrounded by love, she felt his arms encircle her, pull her closer, deepen the kiss until she was breathless, boneless, mindless.

He must love her. He simply must. No man could convey that depth of emotion without feeling the same affection she had been fighting ever since their trip to see Angela. She hadn't realized it then, but she'd started to fall for him almost as soon as he'd shown her his true self.

Kyle slowly released her, studying her expression until she felt the heat rising in her cheeks. "I'm sorry," he said. "I shouldn't have done that."

"Yes, you should," Rachel said boldly. "And if you try to take it back I'll be really disappointed."

"You will?"

"Yes, I will." She stood her ground despite her spinning head and racing pulse. "Unless of course *you* didn't like it."

"Oh, I liked it. I liked it just fine."

It amused her to see high color in his face, too, so she grinned. "Okay. Good. What now?"

He grew even redder. "Um…"

Rachel laughed lightly. "I was referring to taking more precautions and notifying the base again."

"Um, yeah. Right."

"You're cute when you blush," she teased.

"I'm way too old to be cute," Kyle countered. "Besides, officers are not supposed to blush. We're supposed to be all the things that my being here with you negates."

"Would it help your case if I quit the service at the end of my current enlistment?"

"Let's not get ahead of ourselves," he said. "I did have permission to help you so we may skate through."

"Suppose we don't?"

Before Kyle could reply, Stryker sat up. A low rumble began in the K-9's throat and grew to a full growl.

Rachel jumped. Natalie began to cry and ran to her. Kyle strode to the window and scanned the otherwise quiet forest.

"They found us?"

"Not necessarily. It could be a nosy neighbor."

"You can't really believe that."

As she held the frightened child close, Rachel cast around for a safe place to hide her. A one-room cabin didn't provide a lot of options.

She watched Kyle barricade the door by upending a table. "You're not acting like you think it's a neighbor."

"That's because there's more than one person."

"Peter?"

Natalie began to sob against Rachel's shoulder and cling to her neck.

"Maybe. Call the police and tell them to hurry." Kyle displayed a shotgun and half a box of 12-gauge shells. "This is all we have for self-defense."

Rachel made the brief call and stashed Natalie behind the Christmas tree with Stryker, then joined Kyle. "How can I help?"

"You didn't happen to bring a rifle, did you?"

"Nope. And the local sheriff is busy at a multiple-vehicle wreck on the highway so we can't count on him. Do you think they'll attack?"

"Hard to tell. If they don't know we're sitting ducks they may try to wait us out. I don't intend to shoot unless they do." He looked past her. "Where's our girl?"

"Hiding with Stryker." Rachel shivered and rubbed her hands together. "I wrapped her in a blanket but that won't stop a bullet."

"I doubt they'll harm her," Kyle said. "You and I are another matter."

"I'm so sorry I got you into this." There was a catch in her voice.

"If anybody got me into anything it wasn't you," he countered. "I still see this as my second chance to do the right thing. I was absent by choice the first time, when I should have been there for my family. God gave me another opportunity to prove myself."

Was he trying to say he loved her, loved Natalie? Was that even possible? She and Kyle had known each other through work for a couple of years but that wasn't the same as dating. As for her niece, he'd barely met her.

Those facts definitely made them surrogates, she reasoned. This wasn't the only time that premise had occurred to her but it was the first time Kyle had put it into his own words. There was no doubt they needed each other. He needed healing of his spirit, and she needed protection from evil. That was for everyone's good, so how could she argue?

Because I'm selfish, Rachel concluded. When all this was over, perhaps Kyle would still be interested in her. If he wasn't, she'd have to accept it as an unwelcome answer to prayer. Just because she had worked out a pleasing solution in her mind, there was no guarantee God would agree with her plans. The Lord might just as easily see to it that they were separated by air-force protocol and hardly ever saw each other.

That notion brought tears to her eyes and made her want to throw herself into Kyle's arms. Well, she wasn't going to. He needed to be alert, not distracted.

She was searching the cabin for a makeshift weapon when banging on the door startled everyone. Stryker barked. Rachel gasped and froze. Kyle levered a shell into the shotgun.

Whoever was outside must have heard the metallic noise of the slide working, because they stopped pounding.

Rachel peeked through a gap in the curtains. "They're leaving!"

"Not for long, I'm afraid. Get my phone out of my jacket pocket and bring it here. It's high time I called in reinforcements."

As soon as she delivered his phone, she went back to the window and watched four men searching the forest floor.

"Tell them to hurry," she shouted to Kyle. "I think Peter's making a battering ram!"

ELEVEN

"I'll leave my cell connected," Kyle shouted into the phone. "You can home in on it. Just hurry."

"Who's coming?" Rachel asked.

"As many of the K-9 unit as will fit into a small chopper. There's no clearance to land so they'll have to rappel down with their dogs and take the chance of becoming a target."

"It'll take too long for them to drive?"

"A few will fly in while the rest approach from the ground. It's an operation they've trained for."

"How can I help?"

"Stay back, out of the way."

"Not a chance—*Captain*."

"Forget rank and listen to me," Kyle insisted. "You're defenseless. If the bullets start to fly I don't want to worry about you." He jerked his head toward the rear corner. "Get behind the tree with Natalie and Stryker and make sure they stay down, too."

"Is that an order?"

Kyle rolled his eyes. "No, Rachel, it's not. It's a sensible suggestion from someone who cares for you in spite of himself, okay?" To his relief, her resistance gave way to shock, then acquiescence.

"All right. I'll get out of your way. But I won't promise to sit idle if I see you're in danger. Understood?"

Nodding, he figured that was the best he was going to get. Truth to tell, she'd bailed him out before by using her head and not panicking. If he needed help again it was good to know she'd be handy. His biggest problem was letting go of the notion that protecting them all was solely up to him.

Wrong. It's up to God, his thoughts insisted, pushing him to wordless prayer and reminding him of everything he had lost. How could he possibly reconcile those memories with the ones he was making at present? That was asking the impossible, leaving him with the need to place absolute trust in his heavenly Father's decisions. Much of life was beyond understanding for man. Either he believed and relied upon God or he didn't.

As soon as Kyle realized that he needed a different kind of help, he called to Rachel, "Pray. Hard."

He watched as she fell to her knees and pulled Natalie close. They bowed their heads. Kyle joined them in his heart and he gave thanks despite the risk of impending attack.

It was a lot easier to do so on a sunny Sunday morning in the safety of church, which was the point, he guessed. Faith without testing and proving was far too easy to take for granted. So was love.

Rachel let Natalie speak for both of them because the child's prayer was direct and heartfelt instead of being filled with the pat phrases so many adults fell back on when they didn't know what else to say.

"Thank you, Jesus, for saving me from Peter and hug my mommy for me. Please help Auntie Rachel and Kyle. Amen."

The little girl turned misty eyes to Rachel. "Was that okay?"

"It was perfect, honey."

"Good." Rachel let go and Natalie looped both arms around the three-legged dog's neck. "And thank you for Stryker. Amen again."

This was no time for smiles, yet the corners of Rachel's mouth lifted. What a precious little girl. Angela may have failed her in many ways, but the Lord had sent Maria into her life to plant seeds of faith. To take care of His child. Was He using her and Kyle, too? Undoubtedly. All Rachel had to figure out was how to assist without getting in God's way. That had been her error in the past, more times than she cared to count. She had tried to help too much, to do things her way. Listening to Kyle, however, was a different story.

And speaking of listening. She held her breath. Footsteps. Lots of them. On the porch? Yes!

"Brace yourself," Kyle announced. "We're about to be rammed."

Rachel reached for the child, including the K-9 in her embrace. Growls were rumbling, vibrating his chest. "Easy, Stryker. Easy."

Bang! The window panes shook. Dust filtered down from the open rafters. *Bang!*

"It's holding," Kyle shouted.

"What about…" Rachel stopped herself from mentioning the windows. They weren't very big but would probably allow a skinny guy like Peter to wriggle through. How many shotgun shells did they have? Would Kyle fire a warning shot if their attackers chose to come at them that way?

She cast about for a weapon. Anything would do.

There was no poker in the fireplace but there was a blackened iron skillet on the woodstove. If she could reach that and place herself for a strike, she might save a shotgun shell.

Men were stomping around on the narrow porch, arguing and cursing. The moment she overheard one of them say "Window," she put her plan into motion. Cross to the stove, grab the handle of the pan, scurry to the opposite side of the small window without being seen, raise it over her head and wait.

In position, she glanced over at Kyle. He was furious. "Move! I can't shoot with you standing there."

Rachel merely shook her head and held out the pan for him to see, then raised it again. Just in time. The glass shattered. Someone ran a gun barrel along the edges to clear them of sharp points. A hat started to pass through the newly made access.

Every muscle tensing, Rachel forced herself to wait a few moments longer. Almost there. Almost time. *Now!*

Thwack! The iron pan glanced off hat and head, ending up at Rachel's side on the end of her straightened arms. People outside rushed to pull the intruder back and carry him away, all the while shouting and threatening retribution.

Her heart was pounding so rapidly she could hardly separate the beats. A tremor ran up her arms and raced along her spine, leaving her limbs weak and quivering. She met Kyle's astonished gaze. "I—I didn't mean to hit him so hard."

"Forget what I said about you being defenseless. And don't beat yourself up about hurting him. If they get to us they won't be gentle."

Tightening her grip on the handle, she said, "Yeah. That's what I figured."

* * *

Kyle got Rachel to back off by convincing her that their attackers wouldn't try the same approach twice. He still couldn't believe how brave she was. If she judged him in need of her help she was going to provide it, just as she'd promised, whether or not he agreed.

Watching through the unbroken window, he saw a man approaching. His hands were raised and empty, as if he wanted to surrender. That was too good to be true.

Kyle spoke aside to Rachel. "Peter's coming. He looks unarmed but I don't trust him."

"I knew you were smart."

A fist pounded on the door. "Hey, in there. I don't want anybody else to get hurt. Just give me the kid and I'll leave you alone. I swear."

The barrel of the shotgun remained aimed at the closed door. "Don't answer him, Rachel. Let him wonder."

"He should know better than to think I'd ever give up Natalie to him."

"Exactly. He's probably trying to divert our attention while his buddies do something else."

"What?"

"Beats me. I suppose we'll find out. Stay alert."

"Are those the only two windows?"

"Yes." As he scanned the side and rear walls an unusual odor caught his attention. He sniffed, then checked out Stryker. Ears perked, the three-legged K-9 was waving his head back and forth, making use of all his senses.

Apparently Rachel was, too, because she asked, "Do you smell smoke?"

"Yeah. But I don't see anything yet."

She was on the move. "Back here. Look! See it seeping between the logs?"

He certainly did. Soon it would be impossible to

breathe inside, yet if they ventured out, Peter and his cohorts would grab Natalie. The situation was untenable. They couldn't hope to triumph without better weapons.

"I'm not giving up," Kyle declared. "If it gets too bad in here, I'll run out the front shooting so you can slip away with Natalie and Stryker."

"What good will that do? They'll just mow you down and come after us."

"It'll buy you some time."

"And cost you your life. No way."

"Do you have a better idea?"

"Yes. No. I don't know. How about letting them in and taking them on right here? It's cramped but we'd have better control. And Stryker can defend Natalie."

"You mean because they won't be able to sneak behind him. I get it." Kyle had kept the phone connection open. Now he pressed the cell to his ear rather than broadcast their plans. "Security, what's the ETA on that chopper?" His concerned gaze locked with Rachel's and he nodded soberly. "Copy. The sooner the better."

An unasked question lay between them. Kyle led Rachel away from the smoky wall. Stryker was on his feet, standing guard over Natalie while she hugged his ruff. "They're in the air," he told them quietly. "All we need is another five minutes or so. Stay put."

He saw unshed tears in Rachel's eyes as she bent to whisper to her niece. He had to get them out of this somehow. Even if it did cost him his life.

Flames licked up the inside of the logs at the base of the rear wall, leaving wispy fingers of soot. A layer of smoke filled the top half of the room and was slowly dropping lower. Rachel remembered the juice Kyle had mentioned and gathered up an armload of cans to pour over the visible fire. It did seem to help a little. The sound of the battering ram echoed again. Her head ached, her eyes stung and she started to cough. A second trip for more juice took her breath away. They were almost out of options. Almost done. Like it or not, Kyle was going to have to open the door and let in more air. And their enemies. Her duty, then, would be to defend the little girl.

Looking to Kyle and seeing him approaching the door with his shotgun raised, she held her breath. It was getting hard to see, hard to hear, hard to keep the faith.

He reached for the latch, released it and stepped back. In seconds the door burst open and four thugs rushed him. He got off one good shot before they plowed him down. Rachel stood between the child and the melee until one of the men came closer. Then she knocked him flat with her iron frying pan.

Men were shouting. Stryker was barking. The fire, fed by more oxygen, began to crackle and climb the wall. Rachel felt her pulse thrumming, the whoosh in her ears filling the cabin.

Wait! That wasn't her heartbeat; that was the sound of helicopter blades. Help was here!

Anticipation renewed her strength. She covered her head and shoulders with the blanket, scooped up Natalie and ran. By bending over she was able to avoid the thickest smoke and make it to the door. So did Stryker.

The blanket was yanked off her from behind. Peter yelled. Natalie screamed. Stryker launched himself with his powerful hind legs and sank his teeth into their pursuer's shoulder, falling when Peter did but holding on as he'd been trained.

Men and women in full battle dress were rappelling down from a hovering chopper with their K-9 partners. The first pair passed her and burst into the cabin. The second stopped long enough to ask if she and Natalie were okay before joining the charge.

One of the later arrivals gave Stryker the release command and praised him. Rachel didn't care that Peter was bleeding from the bite. It was Kyle she wanted to see. As soon as Stryker hobbled up to her, she ordered him to guard Natalie and ran back toward the smoky cabin.

A simple prayer kept echoing in her thoughts. *Please, God, let Kyle be all right. Please, please, please.*

An airman guarding the space in front of the porch tried to stop her. "I'm sorry, ma'am, you can't come any closer."

"It'll take more than one air-force cop to stop me," she countered.

From behind him came a familiar chuckle. "Better let her by, Sergeant. She swings a mean frying pan."

Rachel had never heard a more welcome sound. "Kyle! I was afraid..." Her voice trailed off as she threw herself at him, wrapped her arms around his waist and held tight. Tears of relief fell freely. At this moment she didn't care who was watching or who might report them. All that mattered was Kyle. He was alive. And he was holding her as if he loved her as much as she loved him. More words could wait. They'd survived and so had the rest of their family: Natalie and Stryker.

Heart overflowing with thanks for deliverance, she clung to the man she adored and let the world go on spinning without further concern. Judging by the way he was embracing her and raining kisses down on the top of her head, Kyle was okay with everything, too. Very okay.

Nevertheless, she needed to hear the words so she took the lead. "I love you, Kyle."

To Rachel's delight he grinned, his eyes filling with emotion, and echoed, "I love you, too."

That was enough for Rachel. For now. And thank God, literally, they would have plenty of time to say a lot more in the future.

EPILOGUE

The annual Christmas party held at the K-9 unit head-quarters included several special guests. General Hall was there to award an official commendation to Stryker for his exemplary work in the field. The proud K-9 accepted his medal on four legs, one of them a custom-made prosthesis. Although it was Kyle Roark who paraded the dog up to the general, little Natalie accompanied them and carefully explained to all present what a hero her new best friend was. Applause rocked the building.

Rachel was so happy and proud she could hardly speak. If someone had told her a few weeks ago what was going to happen in her life, she wouldn't have believed it. God had smoothed out the impassable road and was continuing to do so.

When General Hall followed Kyle, Natalie and Stryker back to the table where Rachel waited, he was all smiles. She mirrored his grin and swiped away a few happy tears as she stood tall and saluted. "Thank you, sir. Thank you for everything."

Hall nodded. "As you were. I'd say *it was my pleasure* if I hadn't had to pull so many strings to keep you out of trouble. You and the doc didn't make my job any easier."

"You went beyond the call of duty when you got Peter

to sign over custody of my niece," Rachel said. "I can't believe he agreed."

"I can be very persuasive when I have to be," the general said.

Kyle laughed nervously. "I hope the same goes for me." He dropped to one knee and took Rachel's hand. "Will you marry me?"

"Yes!" Her eyes jumped to the general, then back to Kyle. "But, how can we? I can't marry my boss without getting us both in trouble, especially you."

"Don't worry. My enlistment is up soon and I'm planning to resume private practice. If you want to stay in the air force we'll just live off the base and you can commute."

So happy she could hardly believe it, Rachel leaned on Kyle's shoulder and sighed. "Okay, but are you sure? I know you love the air force as much as I do."

"I rejoined because I was running away from life," he said. "I had to have God's help forgiving myself and finding a way to move on."

"Sometimes we all do." She snuggled closer. "I wonder if I'll ever be able to forgive Peter."

"He did do two good things," Kyle reminded her. "He brought us together and gave us our first daughter."

Rachel knew she was blushing. "First?"

"God willing." Kyle pulled her into his arms and kissed her under the mistletoe. "Merry Christmas, honey."

Thankful beyond her wildest dreams, she smiled up at him and said, "It certainly is."

* * * * *

Dear Reader,

Memories can cheer us or sadden us, as happened with Rachel and Kyle. Facts don't change but our perception of them can, especially if we accept the past and leave it behind. We may not have control over the acts of others, yet the way we perceive people and events can have a huge effect on us.

Rachel had been abused. She could have withdrawn from life or perhaps repeated the same mistakes. Her faith in God and reliance on Jesus for strength and wisdom helped her break free.

Kyle felt robbed of happiness. He could have stayed bitter, dwelling on his losses, and missed seeing the good right in front of him. Because he trusted God and looked for His providence, he was able to open his heart and love again.

Moving forward is not simple. Sometimes the change seems to take forever. I don't have all the answers but my heavenly Father does. I pray you will seek and find the peace He offers.

Blessings,
Valerie Hansen

"FAST FIVE" READER SURVEY

Your participation entitles you to:
✳ 4 Thank-You Gifts Worth Over $20!

Complete the survey in minutes.

Get 2 FREE Books

See inside for details.

Please help make our
"Fast Five" Reader Survey
a success!

Dear Reader,

Since you are a lover of our books, your opinions are important to us... and so is your time.

That's why we made sure your **"FAST FIVE" READER SURVEY** can be completed in just a few minutes. Your answers to the five questions will help us remain at the forefront of women's fiction.

And, as a thank-you for participating, we'd like to send you **4 FREE THANK-YOU GIFTS!**

Enjoy your gifts with our appreciation,

Pam Powers

To get your
4 FREE THANK-YOU GIFTS:

✷ Quickly complete the "Fast Five" Reader Survey
and return the insert.

"FAST FIVE" READER SURVEY

1 Do you sometimes read a book a second or third time? ○ Yes ○ No

2 Do you often choose reading over other forms of entertainment such as television? ○ Yes ○ No

3 When you were a child, did someone regularly read aloud to you? ○ Yes ○ No

4 Do you sometimes take a book with you when you travel outside the home? ○ Yes ○ No

5 In addition to books, do you regularly read newspapers and magazines? ○ Yes ○ No

YES! I have completed the above Reader Survey. Please send me my 4 FREE GIFTS (gifts worth over $20 retail). I understand that I am under no obligation to buy anything, as explained on the back of this card.

❏ I prefer the regular-print edition 153/353 IDL GM3W

❏ I prefer the larger-print edition 107/307 IDL GM3W

FIRST NAME	LAST NAME

ADDRESS

APT.#	CITY

STATE/PROV.	ZIP/POSTAL CODE

YULETIDE TARGET

Laura Scott

This book is dedicated to Vicki Lynn Christman
and Sally Nowak, two wonderful women who love to read
Love Inspired Suspense books. And of course,
to their beloved Sophie.

Beloved, let us love one another: for love is of God; and every one that loveth is born of God, and knoweth God.

−1 John 4:7

ONE

Senior Airman Jacey Burke felt vulnerable without her K-9 companion, a Belgian Malinois named Greta, as she walked across Canyon Air Force Base toward her apartment. Shivering in the cold December air, she was grateful the darkness was relieved by the string of Christmas lights shimmering merrily up and down Canyon Boulevard.

The back of her neck tingled with awareness and she knew someone was once again watching her.

Curling her fingers around the panic alarm attached to her key ring and nestled in the palm of her hand, she did her best to act nonchalant. In lieu of a weapon, which dog trainers weren't permitted to carry, the panic alarm was the only way she had to protect herself. That and Greta, but unfortunately, rules dictated she kennel her K-9 partner at night.

Waiting at the corner of Canyon and Webster Avenue for the traffic to ease, she resisted the urge to glance back over her shoulder. So far, she hadn't caught anyone watching.

But that didn't mean someone wasn't back there, somewhere.

A large box truck rumbled down Canyon Boulevard,

coming in from the south side of the base. As it approached the intersection, she wrinkled her nose at the rank odor of stale cigarette smoke and sensed someone behind her, a fraction of a second before a strong hand shoved her hard in the center of her back. With a muffled *oomph*, she stumbled forward, directly into the path of the oncoming vehicle.

Her heart lodged in her throat, her chest tightened, making it impossible to scream. It seemed like everything happened in slow motion; her arms pinwheeled as her keys flew from her fingers.

Then her hands slapped hard against the smooth surface of the box truck. Pain rippled up her arms. The force of the blow caused her to spin around like a top. The world tilted dizzyingly before she hit the asphalt with an ungainly thud. She felt the wind against her face as the truck rumbled past, missing her by less than an inch.

Dimly aware of the screeching sound of breaks and the scent of burning rubber, she felt pain reverberate through her body as she lay on the ground, trying to understand what had happened.

"Are you all right?" a deep male voice asked.

She lifted her head to peer up at the man who'd come to her aid, instinctively wary. The man leaning over her looked familiar, but she couldn't quite place him. She blinked, wondering how hard she'd hit her head.

"Jacey Burke?" The man knelt beside her and rested a hand on her shoulder. "Don't move—I'll call an ambulance."

"No, please, don't…" she tried to protest, but it was too late. The man who'd come to her aid had already made the call.

"Did you trip and fall?" His gaze raked over her, as if assessing for blood.

"No." Ignoring his hand on her shoulder, she pushed herself up to a sitting position, wincing at the aches and pains radiating from her hands, arms and knees.

She knew it could have been far worse.

Swallowing the lump in her throat, she scanned the area. "Do you see my keys?"

"Here." He pushed them into her hand.

Fat lot of good her panic alarm had done, she thought with a wry grimace. At least it hadn't shattered to bits.

"Jacey, please. Don't move until the ambulance arrives."

The way he kept calling her by her first name bothered her. She stared through the dim light at his handsome, chiseled features and then belatedly placed him in her memory. "Sean? Sean Morris?"

He smiled and nodded. "It's been a long time, hasn't it?"

"Ten years," she agreed, her mind whirling. She and Sean had attended the same high school back in Branson, Missouri. Sean was a year older, the same age as her brother, Jake.

A wave of sorrow hit hard as she thought about her brother's death in Afghanistan nine months ago. This would be her first Christmas without him.

"What do you mean, no?" Sean asked, interrupting her maudlin thoughts.

She frowned, not understanding at first, until she remembered his earlier question. "No, I didn't trip. I was pushed."

"Pushed? On purpose?" The echo of disbelief in his tone grated on her nerves. She was tired of being treated as if she was losing her mind. Ever since she'd been sent back to base three months ago and reported the strange incidents she'd experienced, she'd heard the whispers.

Cuckoo. Crazy. Delusional.

And knew that's exactly what the person watching her intended.

Not just watching, she mentally corrected herself. Things had escalated beyond discrediting her. Being pushed into the path of an oncoming vehicle was far more serious.

He or she had escalated from trying to make her look crazy to attempting to kill her.

"Hey, is she okay?" A guy dressed as she was in a battle dress uniform came running over. She understood he was the driver of the truck. "I swerved to avoid hitting her."

A move that had likely saved her life.

"I'm Staff Sergeant Morris," Sean said. "I'm a cop, so I'll need to take your statement."

Sean held a rank one level above hers, and she squelched a wave of frustration at her recently denied promotion. She kept her gaze on the truck driver. "Did you see what happened?"

"It looked like you tripped and fell," the driver said.

Jacey swallowed a wave of frustration. "Neither one of you saw anyone behind me? Someone walking away from the corner?"

The two men exchanged a long glance.

"I'm sorry, Jacey, but I didn't notice anyone nearby," Sean admitted. "I was walking in this direction from the parking lot near the south gate, so I didn't have a great view. I only saw the truck swerve seconds before you went flying onto the pavement."

"When I noticed you at the corner, I was already in the process of moving over out of the way when you stumbled forward," the driver said, picking up his side of the story. "I yanked the steering wheel to avoid hitting you. Are you sure you're okay? No broken bones?"

"I'm fine," she insisted, although the bumps and bruises were making themselves known. Her entire body would be sore tomorrow.

"Staff Sergeant, I need to make a delivery to the hospital," the driver said.

"As soon as the ambulance arrives, I'll take your statement for the record," Sean said. "I'm off duty, but as the first cop on the scene, it's my job to make sure this gets reported."

Jacey noticed Sean wasn't dressed in his Special Forces uniform. He was a base cop? And hadn't seen anyone push her into traffic?

She shivered, a cold wave of despair washing over her. If she couldn't get an old high school friend to believe someone had lashed out at her on purpose, who would?

Reeling from seeing Jacey again after all these years, not to mention her allegation of being pushed into the truck's path, Sean did his best to stay focused on the task at hand.

While the EMTs examined Jacey, he nudged the box-truck driver aside. "Name and rank, please," he said, pulling out his notebook.

"Senior Airman Charlie Egan," the driver replied. "I really did my best to avoid hitting her."

"I know," Sean assured him. "If not for your quick reflexes, this could have ended much worse."

"Yeah." Charlie looked somber. "Do you really think she was pushed?"

"No reason not to believe her," Sean said. He fervently wished that he'd seen someone leaving the area where Jacey had been standing, but he hadn't. His entire being had been zeroed in on Jacey's body lying in a crumpled heap on the ground. "You didn't see anyone near her either, correct?"

"Afraid not." Charlie rubbed the back of his neck. "Is it okay if I leave now? I don't want to be late delivering these supplies."

"Sure." Sean tucked his notebook away. "I'll be in touch if I need anything."

"Okay." Charlie loped down the street toward his vehicle.

Sean turned his attention to Jacey Burke, annoyed when he noticed she was pushing the EMTs out of the way.

"I'm fine, see?" She stood and took a few steps. "If I thought I had broken bones, I'd go in for X-rays. But I'm fine."

"Ma'am," one of the EMTs started, but she cut him off.

"I'll sign a waiver. That way you can go help someone who needs it."

"Jacey, you need to go to the hospital," Sean said in a stern tone. "I won't take no for an answer."

Her gaze narrowed. "Really? How will you stop me?"

He glanced at the two EMTs. "Please give us a moment alone." The two EMTs backed off and Sean made sure to lower his voice so that their conversation couldn't be overheard. "You said someone pushed you into the truck's path, correct?"

Her gaze turned wary. "Yes."

"Then I need a hospital report to go along with your allegation so that your injuries are documented."

She appeared to consider his point. "Does this mean you believe me?"

"I have no reason not to," he said, repeating what he'd told the truck driver.

"Fine. I'll go to the ER."

"In the ambulance," he persisted.

She grimaced but reluctantly nodded. "I guess."

"Thanks." He put a hand on her back, gently urging her toward the EMTs. "Airmen? She's ready to go."

When Sean moved away, she grabbed his arm. "Wait. Aren't you coming with me?"

"I'll meet you there," he promised. "I'm going to look over the scene here one more time, then head over to get my car so that I can drive you home."

The warmth of her hand on his arm was distracting. He thought about the way he'd admired her from afar back in high school, then reminded himself that they were different people now.

Especially him. Staying away from his abusive step-father had been his top priority. After his mother's death from cancer, he'd joined the air force and never looked back.

Besides, he wasn't in a good place. Recently, his confidence had taken a hit after the way he'd failed Liz Graber, a woman he'd promised to protect. Her death hung like a dark cloud over him.

The ambulance slowly drove away, and he forced himself to jump into action. He swept the area for clues, but found nothing. He lived in one of the apartments on base but kept his car in a parking area several miles away. He preferred walking while on base but liked having a vehicle handy for those times he needed to get away. He'd moved his grandmother to a small house not far from Canyon and made weekly trips to see her as his schedule allowed. In fact, he'd just returned from a visit with Gram when he'd come across Jacey's collision.

Sean picked up his car and arrived at the base hospital roughly fifteen minutes later. He had to wait another five minutes before they allowed him to see her. Jacey was lying on a gurney, dressed in a hospital gown, her face pale and her dark brown hair falling out of its ponytail. She looked relieved when he stepped into the cubicle.

"They took X-rays and a CT scan of my head. I'm just waiting for the results." She lifted her hands, palms upward. "Just a few scrapes and bruises, nothing more serious. You really needed a hospital visit to go along with the police report?"

"Jacey, if not for the truck driver's quick thinking, you might not even be alive," he reminded her. "It's best to get everything that happened on record so that when we find this guy, we can press the appropriate charges."

She looked as if she wanted to say more, but at that moment, a doctor pushed into the room. "I'm Captain Grant Simons. I reviewed your X-rays and your CT scan—everything looks fine. I suggest you take six hundred milligrams of ibuprofen every six hours for the next two days."

"I will."

Dr. Simons did a quick physical exam, noting the bruises on her knees and the scrapes on her palms. Sean was glad to see the thick fabric of Jacey's battle dress uniform helped protect the skin on her knees; it was obvious her hands had taken the brunt of the collision.

"Am I free to leave now?" Jacey asked.

"Yes. Don't forget to return to the ER if your symptoms get worse."

Jacey nodded and Sean stepped back out of the cubicle to give her privacy to get dressed.

He pulled out his phone to call his boss, Master Sergeant Doug Hanover, but before he could scroll to find the number, Jacey emerged from the room.

"Who are you calling?" she asked sharply.

He was taken aback by her terse tone and slipped his phone into his pocket. "I was going to call my master sergeant, Doug Hanover, but it can wait."

She brushed past him, as if anxious to get out of the hospital. It wasn't until they were outside and settled in his Honda Civic that she turned to look at him. "I'm sure you've heard about me from the other Special Forces cops."

"Um, no, not really." Probably because he'd been preoccupied with how he'd failed Liz Graber. He started the car and waited until she snapped her seat belt into place before backing out of the parking space. "Where do you live? In the base apartment complex on Oakland?"

"Yes, in the south building." She gnawed on her lower lip, as if mentally debating how much more she should tell him. "The report you're going to file tonight isn't the first one. There are a couple of other reports on file from me."

He tightened his grip on the wheel as a flash of frustration toward Jacey surged. "Are you telling me you've been shoved into the path of a truck before?"

"No, that's a first. The previous reports are nothing this serious. Tonight's event has escalated to a whole new level."

Sean tried to relax his grip. "Okay, so what has transpired before tonight?"

"Stupid stuff," she said, waving a dismissive hand. "Like moving my paperwork, hiding my keys, that kind of thing. But I've been trying to get the Special Forces cop I've been dealing with to take my concerns seriously." Her lips thinned. "Maybe after tonight, he will."

"Who have you been working with?"

"Senior Airman Bill Ullman." There was a brief pause, then she said, "I'll be honest—he never believed me. Thought I was making everything up as a way to get attention."

He frowned. "That doesn't make any sense."

"No, it doesn't. I even went over his head to his boss, Master Sergeant Hanover, but he brushed me off, too. And you should also know that I've heard rumors that people think I'm crazy."

"You're not," he instinctively protested.

"Thanks, but you'd be in the minority thinking that." There was a hint of bitterness in her tone.

He pulled up in front of the same apartment complex he lived in and put the gearshift into Park. "Why don't you tell me why someone is trying to hurt you?"

She shook her head helplessly for a moment, staring out her passenger-side window. Then she sighed and turned to face him. "I guess you'll find out sooner or later."

He nodded, waiting for her to continue.

"I've been back on Canyon Air Force Base since October, but prior to that, Greta and I were deployed in Kabul, Afghanistan. Greta is a bomb-sniffing dog and our job was to find IEDs before they could injure any members of the military. Greta and I worked tirelessly for six months, finding close to fifty buried bombs. I was called in to speak to Lieutenant Colonel Ivan Turks for what I assumed would be a promotion."

He inwardly tensed, sensing a promotion was not on the agenda.

"The time of the meeting was nineteen hundred hours, long after his office staff were gone for the day. The lieutenant colonel attempted to assault me." Her tone was flat, as if she were reciting from the air force handbook instead of an act of violence. "I managed to get away before he succeeded, and when I heard Greta and I were denied our promotion, I filed charges against him."

"I'm sorry to hear that you had to go through that," Sean said in a low voice. "I'm sure it wasn't easy, but I'm glad you filed charges. Too many women wouldn't have had the courage."

"Yeah, well I can understand why. Because it became a he-said-she-said scenario. My allegation was deemed *not credible*." She used her fingers to put air quotes around the phrase.

His gut clenched. "Why?"

"Because the lieutenant colonel was able to eliminate any evidence that he requested the meeting in his office. His story was that I came in uninvited and made a move on him in an effort to secure my promotion."

"That's ridiculous!"

"I know. But it doesn't matter. Greta and I were sent back to base as if we'd done something wrong." She was silent for a long moment before she lifted her gaze to his. "I believe that being pushed into oncoming traffic was a way to silence me, forever."

Sean sat back, stunned by her theory. As a cop, he needed to consider all options. It didn't make much sense that a lieutenant colonel would try to kill a lowly senior airman over an allegation that wasn't even taken seriously.

But if this recent attack on Jacey wasn't connected to Turks, then what was it related to?

Who hated her enough to kill her?

TWO

Jacey hated reliving the moment when Lieutenant Colonel Turks roughly grabbed her and tried to force himself upon her. The stale scent of cigarette smoke was still enough to make her gag. If not for her older brother Jake's insistence on teaching her self-defense, coupled with her basic training, she may not have gotten away unscathed.

She swallowed hard, shoving the memory aside. At least Sean believed her, maybe because he'd known her back in high school.

Ten years that seemed like ten lifetimes ago.

"Who else knows about your allegations against Turks?"

"Who doesn't?" She did her best to hide the bitterness in her tone. "I'm sure the notification went into my file, flagging me as a troublemaker. I could tell because when I first arrived at the training center, Master Sergeant Westley James wasn't thrilled to be saddled with me. Thankfully, he's mellowed a bit since then, because I'm getting good results with the K-9s I'm training."

"Lieutenant Colonel Turks isn't on base, too, is he?" Sean asked.

She shook her head. "No, he's still in Kabul." It made her sick to think about how Turks may have already found his next victim.

Doubtful she was the first or the last. It only took a few bad officers to taint what most considered a noble profession.

Serving their country.

"Hard to believe that he could set up an attack on you from Afghanistan."

Her hopes of being believed quickly deflated. "I know." She unlatched her passenger-side door. "Thanks for the ride."

"Wait." Sean snagged her arm, preventing her from leaving. "I'm not saying I don't believe you, Jacey. I'm only thinking out loud here. Anyone sympathetic to Turks could be involved."

"Not just sympathetic to him," she argued. "It would take more than mere sympathy to attempt to kill me." And people thought she was nuts?

Trying to kill her—that was truly insane.

"You're right," he agreed. "I'll keep that in mind as I continue to investigate."

She glanced at him. "As much as I'd like that, you need to know Senior Airman Bill Ullman is the Special Forces cop assigned to my case. Master Sergeant Hanover wouldn't replace him."

"So you said. But since I was on the scene tonight, I'll pressure Hanover to let me take the case over. He'd have no reason not to."

She hoped he was right. Bill Ullman had made no secret of the fact that he didn't like her and didn't believe her. Then again, neither did Hanover.

No one did. Except for Sean.

"Any chance you'd be willing to stay in a motel off base for the night? I'd rather know for sure you're safe."

"I can't." It was odd, but despite the fact that she'd narrowly escaped harm from the earlier incident, she'd feel even more vulnerable off base. "I have to work in the morning, and besides, I don't own a car. Getting back and forth via taxi would be pricey."

Sean grimaced, then nodded. "Okay, I get it." He reached into the glove box and pulled out a small service weapon. "Stay put for a second. I'll walk you inside."

She knew that Sean was just being extra cautious, but it was nice to have him at her side as they approached the apartment building. The scent of his woodsy aftershave made her keenly aware of him.

Knock it off, she told herself sternly. Getting involved with Sean wasn't an option. He was putting his career on the line just by associating with her. Expecting anything more than friendship would be ludicrous.

They took the stairs to the third floor. "Do you live in the complex, too?" she asked.

"Yeah, but in the north building and on the fourth floor." Sean held the door at the top of the stairwell open for her. "Which unit is yours?"

"Three-ten." Outside her door, she pulled out her keys, but Sean took them from her fingertips.

"Stand behind me." He unlocked her door, then pushed it open. He entered the apartment first, weapon ready as he cautiously entered, making sure it was safe. She followed close behind, a little embarrassed at the small, crooked tree sitting on her kitchen table. No real trees were allowed due to the potential fire hazard.

And since Jake's passing, she'd found it difficult to get into the Christmas spirit.

"Thanks for the lift," she said, as Sean returned to the main living area, tucking his weapon away.

"You're welcome. Do me a favor and take down my number. Call me anytime for any reason, okay?"

Taking his phone number seemed a bit personal, but

she reluctantly pulled out her phone and dutifully entered Sean as a new contact. "Got it."

He held his phone, looking at her expectantly, as if waiting for her number, too. She told herself to stop making such a big deal out of it and provided her number in return.

"Thanks." He entered the information, then scanned the room with a frown. "I don't like leaving you here, alone."

Truthfully, she wasn't fond of the idea, either. "I was thinking of calling my boss at the training center, Master Sergeant Westley James, to see if he'd give me special permission to keep Greta here with me 24/7. When the Red Rose Killer, Boyd Sullivan, was on the loose, K-9s were allowed special dispensation to stay with their handlers. After Boyd was captured and arrested last month, the rules went back to normal." She shrugged. "I figure Westley might grant me permission."

"I like it." He gestured with his hand. "Call him."

Bothering the master sergeant at home went against the grain, but remembering that moment when a hand shoved her in the back and directly into traffic had her making the call.

The phone rang several times, then went to voice mail. She left a message, then disconnected from the call.

"Do you think he'll get back to you tonight?"

"If he can, he will." She knew Westley's wife, Felicity, was about three months pregnant and suffering severe morning sickness. Westley was likely taking care of her. As he should. It was up to her to deal with her own problems.

"I'll stick around for a while," Sean offered. "I don't mind sleeping on your sofa. Or if you'd be more comfortable, you can sleep on my sofa."

"Not necessary." Just the thought of having Sean sleep on her sofa or vice versa was enough to wreak havoc on her concentration. He was clueless about the secret crush she'd had on him back in high school. He'd been cute then and had grown more handsome since. But her feelings were one-sided. Back then, he'd never seemed to notice her other than as the kid sister of his friend.

"Really, Sean, you've already gone above and beyond. I'll be fine."

He didn't look convinced, his blue eyes drilling into hers as if trying to read her mind. "There's nothing more important than keeping you safe."

She appreciated his concern. "I'm safe here. I'm going to take some ibuprofen and get some sleep," she said firmly. "Good night."

"Good night." He finally moved to the door. "Don't forget to call if you need something."

"I won't." She waited until he stepped into the hallway, then closed and locked the door behind him. Shooting the dead bolt home made her feel a little better. Then she toured her apartment, making sure each window was securely locked.

Good thing it was winter. In the spring and fall she preferred to sleep with the windows open.

Even with the Christmas tree, the apartment seemed hollow and lonely without Greta or Sean's presence. She set the phone near her bedside table, hoping Westley would call her back. She washed her face and changed out of her uniform into soft black stretch pants and a fleece shirt. Then she crawled into bed and tried to rest.

Images from the truck incident whirled around in her head, causing her to relive the moment over and over again.

It didn't take long to regret her knee-jerk reaction of

refusing Sean's help. What would it have mattered if he'd slept on her sofa? She wasn't going to get any sleep this way, either.

She couldn't understand why someone wanted her dead. This all had to be related to her attempt to file charges against Lieutenant Colonel Turks. And it still irked her that she'd been denied the promotion.

Not just for herself but for Greta's sake. As with all dog handlers, Greta carried the same rank she did. Greta hadn't been given any recognition for the bomb-sniffing work she'd done overseas. They'd both put their lives on the line over and over again to keep their fellow airmen and other members of the military safe.

And as a result, not only were they denied a promotion, but now there'd been an attempt to kill her.

A faint sound had her bolting upright in bed, her heart pounding with fear. It was nothing—just the sound of an apartment door closing.

She couldn't seem to relax, tossing and turning relentlessly. The hours ticked by slowly: 2200, 2300.

At midnight, she gave up and rolled out of bed. She decided to head over to the training center to pick up Greta. She could explain everything to Westley in the morning. Surely, he wouldn't hold it against her, especially if she explained about the recent attempt on her life.

Spurred into action, she pulled on a quilted jacket and slipped out of her apartment, squinting in reaction to the brightly lit hallway. Taking the stairs to the first floor, she pushed through the heavy door into the darkness outside.

Belatedly, she wondered if she should have called Sean, then ruthlessly shoved the cowardly thought aside. The person who'd shoved her into traffic wouldn't find her such an easy target next time. And as an added precaution, she once again palmed the panic button. If she so much as saw anything suspicious, she wouldn't hesitate to make a lot of noise.

As she headed down Oakland, a shiver of apprehension rippled down her spine. This time, she purposefully glanced over her shoulder, letting anyone who might be watching know that she was on full alert.

But, of course, she didn't see anyone.

Stupid to be so afraid. Her schedule at the training center wasn't a secret. It wouldn't be difficult to figure out she reported each morning at 0900 and worked until 1800. No one could possibly know that she was making a midnight run to fetch her K-9 partner.

She squared her shoulders and picked up the pace until she was moving at a steady jog. *Just like being back in basic training*, she thought with a grim smile. Getting her blood moving also warmed her up, and she became even more determined to bring Greta back to her apartment for what remained of the night.

Fifteen minutes later, she reached the training center and the row of kennels along the back. She walked along the dimly lit hallway, refusing to let anything deter her from her mission.

As she moved down the corridor, she mentally counted the kennels as she passed by, knowing Greta was in number seventeen.

She approached Greta's kennel cautiously. Her K-9 partner was well trained, but she was also a warrior.

It didn't hurt to be careful.

Crouching beside Greta's kennel, she peered through the metal bars. The Belgian Malinois lifted her head, and her tail thumped with recognition, but she didn't seem to be her usual self.

"Greta?" Her tone caused several of the other dogs to

bark. Ignoring them, she quickly unlocked the door and went into the kennel.

"What's wrong, girl?" She frowned as she noted a small puddle of green fluid staining the bottom of Greta's empty water dish.

Antifreeze?

No! She pulled out her phone and dialed the emergency veterinary service, surprised when Captain Kyle Roark himself answered the phone.

"Dr. Roark," he answered in a voice husky with sleep.

"It's Jacey Burke. Greta is sick—I think she's been poisoned with antifreeze."

"What? How did that happen? Never mind—I'll meet you at the clinic," he said, all traces of slumber erased from his tone.

"I'll bring her right away."

Jacey stuffed her phone in her pocket and then bent over Greta, who was struggling to stand. The dog weighed roughly seventy pounds, but that didn't stop Jacey from hauling Greta up and into her arms. Surging to her feet, she staggered out of the kennel and hurried down the corridor.

Fearing for Greta's well-being, she prayed for strength as she carried her K-9 partner to the veterinary clinic. If she hadn't decided to come out tonight… She could barely finish the thought.

First someone tried to kill her, then they went after her K-9 partner.

She was afraid to think about what this guy might do next.

THREE

Sean's ringing phone instantly pulled him from a restless slumber. When he squinted at the screen and saw Jacey's name, his heart jumped into his throat. Levering upright, he quickly answered. "Jacey? What's wrong?"

"I-I'm at the veterinary clinic. S-someone poisoned Greta." Jacey's voice was thick with tears. "Dr. Roark is doing his best, but I'm afraid sh-she won't make it."

"I'll be right there. Don't leave, okay?"

"I won't."

Sean pulled on his uniform, including his utility belt and his weapon, just in case, before bolting out of the apartment. He wondered how Jacey had known that Greta was poisoned. It didn't matter, because he'd get a statement from the vet regardless, but there was a tiny portion of his mind that wondered if Jacey was blowing things out of proportion.

Maybe the dog was simply sick. And why was Jacey at the kennel at this late hour, anyway? He didn't truly believe she was crazy, but there was no doubt her behavior could be viewed as a bit erratic.

He debated waiting for a cab or just going on foot. Because the veterinary clinic wasn't that far, he opted for the latter. He quickened his pace to double time, heading up Oakland past the now-vacant children's playground toward Canyon Drive.

The lights were on at the clinic, but the door was locked. He rapped on the window and watched Jacey cautiously approach to answer the door. Her eyes were red and puffy, her cheeks damp with tears.

"Thanks for coming," she said in a husky tone, closing the door behind him.

Hating to see her so upset, he drew her into his arms for a brief, friendly hug. "Any news on Greta's condition?"

She leaned against him for a moment, the cranberry-vanilla scent of her hair teasing his senses, then straightened and shook her head. "Not yet. I can't believe anyone would be so cold and callous as to go after my dog."

"Why were you at the kennel tonight?"

She dragged a hand through her hair. "I couldn't sleep and thought it would help to bring Greta to my place for the rest of the night. I hadn't heard back from Master Sergeant Westley James, but thought I could ask forgiveness in the morning. If I hadn't gone to get Greta she may have died."

He had to admit her story sounded reasonable. But he continued, choosing his words carefully. "You mentioned something about her being poisoned?"

"I saw a small puddle of green fluid that appeared to be antifreeze in the bottom of her water dish." Jacey rubbed her hands over her arms, as if chilled. "Antifreeze tastes sweet so dogs and other animals are attracted to it, but it's extremely poisonous. I can guarantee there's no way even a smidgen of antifreeze got into the kennel by accident." Her gaze darkened. "Someone put it there on purpose."

"I'd like to see it for myself, maybe take pictures." He

knew she wouldn't want to leave the veterinary clinic, but this was important. "Why don't you let Dr. Roark know we'll be back in twenty minutes? That should be long enough for me to get a sample of the antifreeze for my report."

She hesitated, torn between being there for Greta and helping to catch the person who'd done this terrible thing. She reluctantly nodded and moved over to the exam room. "Dr. Roark? Can you hear me?"

A pretty blonde poked her head into the room. "Is there something you need?"

"Hi, Airman Fielding. Just tell Dr. Roark I'll be back in roughly twenty minutes. The Special Forces cop wants to see the scene of the crime."

The woman nodded. "Okay. Don't worry, Kyle—er, Dr. Roark is doing everything he can for Greta."

"I know. Thanks again." Jacey turned away and faced him. "Let's go."

They left the veterinary clinic together. He was glad he had some evidence containers stored in the pocket of his utility belt. Having a sample of the antifreeze that had poisoned Greta would go a long way in proving her case that someone was trying to kill her and her K-9 partner.

Jacey didn't say anything as they hurried down Canyon to the training center. She used her key to access the building and then took him down a long corridor lined with kennels housing a variety of dogs. Several of them barked as they walked past, but Jacey acted as if she didn't notice.

"It's this one," she said, slowing to stop. She frowned, sweeping her gaze around the area. "That's odd. I'm sure I left the kennel door open. I was in a hurry to get Greta to the clinic so didn't bother trying to close it behind me."

He knelt down and peered through the thin metal bars

of the kennel door to see inside. There was a steel water dish in the far corner but no sign of antifreeze.

"Are you sure this is the right kennel?" he asked.

"Of course I'm sure." Jacey used her key to unlock the kennel door and ducked inside. Then she stopped abruptly, staring in confusion. "The water dish has been cleaned up. There's no sign of the antifreeze in the bottom that I noticed earlier."

A sinking feeling settled in his gut. "You're sure you saw it?"

"Absolutely." She lifted her gaze to his. "Someone came in to clean up after I left with Greta."

He nodded, wondering who had access to the kennels. "Any way to track who has been in and out of here?"

Her shoulders slumped in defeat. "All the trainers and staff have keys. Unfortunately, there isn't an electronic trail. But Greta is trained not to take food or water from strangers, which makes me wonder if the person who did this is someone who works here."

"Is it possible someone followed you in and stayed hidden until you left with Greta? That would give them plenty of time to wash out the water dish."

"Maybe," she admitted, although her tone reeked of doubt. She slowly walked out of the kennel. "It's possible Greta drank the antifreeze because the dish was in her kennel. We can't always have the same staff providing food and water. Either way, I'm sure Dr. Roark will be able to verify the source of Greta's illness."

Sean followed her back outside, watching as she closed and relocked the kennel door. Hopefully she was right about that.

Because if the vet couldn't say with absolute certainty what the source of Greta's illness was, they only had

Jacey's account of what she'd seen when she'd found Greta in her kennel.

And at this rate, Sean was concerned that no one would be willing to believe her.

If he hadn't seen her almost get run over by the box truck, he wasn't so sure he would, either.

But he did believe her. And not just because they'd known each other back in high school.

Jacey truly cared about Greta and wouldn't make something like this up.

Despite the efforts of someone trying to prove otherwise.

What they needed was a suspect. But who? Out of the thousands of airmen and officers on base, who would hate Jacey enough to attempt to kill her and her dog?

He wasn't sure but intended to find out. He couldn't bear the thought of another woman being attacked on base. Four weeks ago, he'd failed to keep Liz Graber safe from her abusive ex-husband. Liz's death was his fault. All because he'd gotten too emotionally involved and had let his guard down.

No way was he going to fail to protect Jacey Burke.

Jacey sensed Sean was struggling to believe she had seen antifreeze in Greta's kennel.

At this point, she was even beginning to doubt herself.

Worse, Sean only had her word about what she'd seen. By now he was likely wondering if the rumors about her being crazy were in fact true. She had to believe Dr. Roark would support her story.

"I didn't make it up," she said, finally breaking the tangible silence between them as they made their way back to the veterinary clinic.

"I believe you," Sean said, surprising her.

"Really?"

"Yes, really."

There was more she wanted to say, but they had already reached the veterinary clinic. She rapped on the door, grateful to see through the window that Airman Fielding had come over to let them in. The veterinary tech greeted them both with a weary smile.

"Dr. Roark has Greta stable for the moment. He'll be out in a few minutes to talk to you."

Jacey's heart swelled with hope. "That's good, right?"

"Yes, it's good. For now." Airman Fielding nodded, then disappeared into the back of the clinic.

Sean reached for her hand, and she gratefully took it, drawing comfort from his warmth.

He believed her. She wasn't sure why, but he believed her.

The relief made tears prick her eyes. Ridiculous, but hearing those three little words made her feel so much better.

"Senior Airman Burke?" Dr. Roark approached, eyeing Sean curiously.

She let go of Sean's hand and offered a quick salute. "Captain Roark, this is Staff Sergeant Sean Morris. He's with the Special Forces."

Sean also saluted, as was required when facing a superior officer.

Captain Roark returned their salutes, then waved a hand. "At ease, both of you. No need to be formal here." The vet looked at her. "I've managed to stabilize Greta, but at the moment the biggest threat is to her kidneys. Depending on how much she took in, she'll need time for her system to return to normal."

Jacey asked, "But she'll survive?"

Captain Roark nodded. "Yes, her prognosis is very

good. Most dogs can survive antifreeze poisoning if they get treatment right away. I plan to keep her here for at least twenty-four hours for observation." His gaze grew troubled. "It's good you brought her in when you did, Jacey—if this had waited until morning, she likely wouldn't have survived."

A cold fist squeezed her heart and she nodded. "I know. I believe God was watching over both of us tonight."

"You're right about that."

"Captain, may I ask a few questions?" Sean asked, pulling out his notebook.

Dr. Roark frowned. "It's the middle of the night. Can this wait until morning?"

"I understand. How about just one statement from you verifying that Jacey's K-9, Greta, was indeed poisoned by antifreeze."

The vet hesitated. "I can't say that with absolute certainty at this time. Jacey was the one who noticed the antifreeze—I simply treated Greta accordingly. She does have kidney failure, which is a key finding in antifreeze poisoning, but testing for ethylene glycol isn't as simple as doing a toxicology screen—it's far more complicated. At this point, all I'm willing to say is that it appears Greta was poisoned."

Jacey couldn't believe what the vet was saying. No way to prove for sure? No way to tell with absolute certainty that Greta was poisoned with antifreeze?

How was it possible? She couldn't bear to think about the person who'd tried to kill Greta actually getting away with it.

"But there is a blood test that can be done to prove it, right?" Sean pressed.

Captain Roark nodded. "There is, and I have drawn a

sample, but need to send it out to the San Antonio crime lab for further analysis."

"I totally agree." Sean closed his notebook and stuffed it back in his pocket. "In fact, I'll swing by in the morning to pick it up to take it personally, if that's okay."

"Fine with me." Captain Roark yawned. "Good night."

"Good night." Jacey forced the words past her tight throat. She released Sean's hand and blindly turned toward the door.

"Jacey." Sean's voice was low and husky as he caught her arm. "Don't give up hope, okay? We'll prove what happened here."

"You can't be sure of that." She wrenched away, pushed open the door and stepped out into the frigid night air. Not only was she forced to return to her apartment alone, but there was once again the chance that her version of what happened to Greta wouldn't be deemed credible.

It was as if everything that had transpired with the lieutenant colonel was happening all over again.

And she couldn't help wondering if she wouldn't be better off leaving the air force for good.

Sean hated seeing Jacey so upset. He hurried to catch up with her, determined not to let her go anywhere alone.

"Jacey, wait." His sharp tone made her pause and glance at him over her shoulder. "We need a game plan."

"What are you talking about?" she asked impatiently. "There's nothing more to be done at zero two thirty in the morning."

"If you were followed into the kennel tonight, which is likely since we know someone cleaned up the antifreeze after you left, it's not safe for you to go back to your apartment." He took her elbow in his hand and steered her straight down Canyon, toward the small parking lot where he'd left his car. "You need to stay somewhere off base tonight."

"No, I don't." She dug in her heels. "It's too far away and I have to be at the training center first thing so I can explain all of this to my boss."

"You can do that over the phone," he insisted. "Are you willing to put the other K-9s in harm's way?"

That caused her to whirl around to stare at him. "You think my presence alone puts them in danger?"

He sighed, unwilling to lie to her. "I don't know— it's not likely. There are a lot of staff around, especially during the daytime hours. Still, why not call off sick for the day until we have a handle on what happened here?"

It was clear she didn't like that suggestion.

"Listen, my car is parked just up the block. Let's just get off base and find a motel room. If you won't take off the whole day, at least tell your boss that you'll be in later, say around noon."

She narrowed her gaze. "But I'm not sick."

"No, but you were almost run over by a truck." Her stubbornness was starting to annoy him. "One late start isn't going to be the end of the world. I'm sure your boss will understand."

Her shoulders slumped as if she were abruptly slammed with a wave of exhaustion. "Okay, fine. But you're coming with me to talk to Westley. He'll want to know what you and your team are going to do to ensure the safety of all the K-9s. This is the last thing he needs right now, considering everything Boyd Sullivan did while sneaking on and off base. Boyd wasn't just the Red Rose Killer—he let all the dogs loose, along with attacking and killing personnel he'd targeted with a red rose. Not to mention killing people who simply got in his way. After months of havoc, Westley wants things to return to normal, especially with the upcoming Christmas holiday."

Sean nodded, relieved she'd finally given in. "Not a problem."

There was a lot of work he needed to do on Jacey's case. Two reports still had to be filed, one on the truck collision and the other on Greta's possible poisoning. Not to mention bringing his boss up to speed on everything that had transpired.

Lastly, he wanted to get copies of the other reports Jacey had filed with Senior Airman Bill Ullman.

Sean wanted to dig into the case immediately, but knew that he needed to start with a phone call to his boss first thing in the morning.

Right now, Jacey's safety was his only priority.

As they approached the parking lot, he slowed his steps, realizing that several of the streetlights were out.

The tiny hairs on the back of his neck lifted in warning. He reached for Jacey's arm and tugged her close. "I don't like this," he muttered. "The two lights on either side of the parking lot were working earlier. Now they're both out?"

"Maybe we should return to the apartment," Jacey whispered.

He wasn't keen on that idea, especially if they were being followed. "After everything that's transpired, I think getting off base is the better option."

The muffled sound of gunfire echoed through the night, followed by a burning sensation along his upper arm. Reacting instinctively, Sean grabbed Jacey and yanked her over toward the closest vehicle, dropped to the ground and used it for cover.

"Are you hit?" he asked anxiously.

"No. You?"

"I'm good." His arm felt like it was on fire, but he knew it was little more than a flesh wound. He looked around, trying to figure out which direction the gunshots had come from. Not directly in front of them, maybe to the north east? Using his body to shield Jacey, he fumbled for his phone, desperate to get backup to their location, *now*.

If the shooter had night-vision goggles, they were sitting ducks out here.

The next couple of moments could very well be their last.

FOUR

For the second time in a matter of hours, Jacey felt the rough asphalt against the palms of her hands. She held her breath, her heart thudding in her chest as fear cloaked her. What was going on? Sean had her pressed against the ground, his body covering hers. She listened as he spoke to the dispatcher, requesting backup to the parking lot near the south gate because of a shooter in the area.

Shooter? Gunshots? The sounds hadn't seemed loud enough for gunfire. While deployed in Afghanistan she'd heard plenty, all of it loud enough to make her ears ring for hours afterward.

"Backup is on the way," Sean said, his voice low and husky near her ear.

"You're sure someone was shooting at us?"

"Yes, I'm sure. I believe the gunman used a silencer."

Hearing the grim determination in Sean's tone made her stomach twist painfully.

Sean was in danger now, too. Because he believed in her.

She hated knowing that she'd dragged him into her mess. Was this really all because she'd reported the lieutenant colonel?

It was hard to comprehend why someone on base cared

enough about her allegation to try to kill her. That someone hated her enough to risk taking a Special Forces cop down, too.

"Do you think the shooter is gone?" she whispered.

"No idea, but we're staying put." The wail of sirens echoed through the night. Jacey thought that if the perp hadn't left by now, he or she no doubt would after hearing proof that help was on the way. "Once we have the scene secured, we'll look for evidence. I'm sure there are shell casings or bullets somewhere."

She nodded, wishing Greta was here. Her K-9 partner had a great nose for finding the scent of gunpowder. Bombs were her specialty, but during training sessions, Jacey had tested Greta with bullets, as well. Greta had been incredibly accurate with even the smallest-size bullet, like those from a 0.22.

Red-and-blue flashing lights grew bright as additional Special Forces cops arrived. Sean didn't let her up, though, until they were approached by two cops holding their weapons at the ready.

"Staff Sergeant Morris?" one of them asked. "You reported two gunshots?"

"Yes, I did." Sean straightened and then held out his hand to help her up. "This is Senior Airman Jacey Burke."

"Staff Sergeant Cronin," the cop introduced himself. "What happened?"

"This is the third attempt to harm Senior Airman Burke in less than eight hours." Sean's voice was terse. "Earlier tonight someone shoved her in front of a truck, then her K-9 partner, Greta, was poisoned with antifreeze. I was planning to take her off base when I realized the two streetlights were out over the parking lot where I left my car."

Staff Sergeant Cronin glanced up to see for himself, and frowned.

"I suspected something was wrong," Sean continued, "but before we could move, I heard gunfire and felt a bite of pain along my upper arm. We dove for cover and called it in."

"You're hit?" Jacey brushed her hand along the side of his shoulder, appalled to find her fingers wet and sticky with blood. "Why didn't you say something?"

"I'm fine." Sean brushed off her concern. "The gunman used a silencer. I heard two distinct shots before I was hit. They came in from the northeast. We need to search the area, find the spent shell casings or bullet fragments."

"We'll take a look around," Staff Sergeant Cronin promised. "I'll call the EMTs over to provide medical attention."

"Don't bother," Sean said at the same time Jacey replied, "Yes, that would be good."

Staff Sergeant Cronin nodded at Jacey. "I agree with Senior Airman Burke. That wound needs attention."

"My arm doesn't matter—getting Senior Airman Burke to safety does."

"You'll both be safe enough in the ER for a while." The staff sergeant wasn't taking no for an answer. "You should call Master Sergeant Hanover to let him know what's happened. I'll get the EMTs over here."

"Your turn to make sure this gets documented by the ER doctors," Jacey murmured. It was a lame attempt at a joke.

"I guess." Sean didn't look happy.

Twenty minutes later, they were in a different ER cubicle. Ironically, the same ER doctor, Captain Grant Simons, came in to examine Sean's wound. The skin was furrowed where the bullet had skimmed by, and staring at it made Jacey feel sick at how close she'd come to losing Sean. A few inches more, and he'd be lying on an operating-room table, or worse.

Jacey took a seat in the corner of the room and dropped her head into her hands. Then she lifted her heart in prayer.

Heavenly Father, thank You for sparing Sean's life, and I ask that You please continue to keep us safe. Please help Greta heal from her ordeal, too. Amen.

Another thirty minutes passed before a nurse came in to clean the wound and bandage it. Sean never uttered a complaint, even though she knew the jagged wound running across his biceps had to hurt.

At nearly five in the morning, Sean was officially discharged from care. They were getting ready to leave when Sean's phone rang. He pulled it out and grimaced. "My boss returning my earlier call," he said, before answering. "This is Staff Sergeant Morris."

Jacey wished she could hear the other side of the conversation.

"Yes, sir, I'm fine but Senior Airman Jacey Burke was the real target here and I need a safe place to go for the next few days. We both live in apartment housing and that's not secure enough."

Jacey didn't believe she was the shooter's only target; Sean had been the one injured, not her.

"A motel is one option. I may have another one. I'll keep you posted." He disconnected from the call and looked at Jacey. "I'm going to see if there's a vacant house we can use for a week or so."

"I thought base housing was only for officers and difficult to get?"

"It is, but I happen to know of a place where a family moved out rather unexpectedly. I know it will get reassigned, but I'm hoping we can use it for a limited time."

She narrowed her gaze. "You just happen to know this?"

"Yeah. I, uh, looked into alternative housing options when you refused to go off base to a motel."

She nodded, understanding his concern. If there was a house available to use, they should jump on it. It was far more preferable than a motel off base.

Sean made two more quick calls, then returned to her side. "Everything is all set. We can use the place for five days. Ready to go?" Sean asked, shrugging into his jacket. The sleeve had a rip in it where the bullet had torn through.

"Yes." She rose to her feet, feeling exhausted. "I need to shower and change before returning to the training center to talk to my boss about Greta."

"We'll take a cab to the apartment to pick up a few things, then grab a different cab to head over to pick up the key and take us to the house," Sean said. "I want to be certain we're not followed."

"All right," she agreed. "Let's go."

Jacey couldn't relax during the cab ride to the apartment complex. Sean sat sideways in his seat so he could keep an eye on the road behind them. Even at 0500 hours, Canyon Air Force Base had come to life. Military personnel started work early.

"Is there anyone behind us?" she asked.

"Too many," he replied glumly. He tapped the cab driver on the shoulder. "Will you circle the block?"

The cabbie shrugged. "It's your dime."

Jacey breathed easier once they managed to get into her apartment without incident. Sean waited for her in the living room, giving her time to shower and change. She quickly packed a bag, then rejoined him in the living room. "I'm set."

"Good." His smile didn't reach his eyes, and she knew he was troubled by the back-to-back incidents from that night. "My turn."

They used the side exit, avoiding the main areas, to walk over to Sean's building. He couldn't get his dressing wet, so he simply changed his clothes and packed a bag. He wore his official uniform, complete with the blue beret, and a wide utility belt that held a holster for his gun.

She thought he was handsome before, but wearing his full uniform he stole her breath.

Doing her best to hide her reaction, she kept her gaze averted as a different cabbie drove them to the small house off Webster, not far from the base apartment-housing complex. She could see the apartment building from the front window.

"Let me know when you're ready to head over to the training center," Sean said. "I'd like to talk to the staff who were on duty over the past twenty-four hours, see if they noticed anything unusual."

"Uh, sure. I'm ready." Jacey abruptly realized just how much time she and Sean would be spending together. He'd been nothing but professional, but ever since she'd seen the wound on his arm up close, not to mention seeing him in his full uniform, she'd found herself getting emotionally involved on a personal level.

She'd had a crush on him ten years ago, but that was then. This was now.

Best to figure out how to rein in her feelings before she made a complete and utter fool of herself.

* * *

Sean sensed Jacey was on edge as they took a third taxi to the training center.

"This is going to get expensive," Jacey muttered as he paid the fare.

She was right, but there wasn't anything he could do to change that right now. He didn't dare use his personal vehicle, but planned to sign out a jeep from the base motor pool.

"Did you call your master sergeant?" he asked as they entered the facility.

"Not since I left him a message about Greta's condition, but I'm sure he's looking for me." She led the way to the office area. "I hope he doesn't blame me for this."

"He won't," Sean said in an attempt to reassure her.

Jacey didn't look convinced, and knocked sharply on the door of the corner office.

"Come in."

Jacey grimaced and opened the door. She went in first and, while saluting wasn't required, stood at attention. Sean did the same, waiting until Master Sergeant James told them to stand at ease before relaxing.

"Take a seat. What happened, Jacey?" Master Sergeant James asked, his expression full of concern.

Sean listened as Jacey repeated the events surrounding Greta's poisoning. When he sensed she was going to leave it there, he interrupted.

"Sir? If I may interject here—" he paused and waited for Westley to nod "—there have been two attempts against Jacey over the last twenty-four hours along with the attack on her K-9 partner."

"Who are you?"

Oops. "Staff Sergeant Sean Morris with Special Forces, sir. I came to offer first aid to Senior Airman

Burke after she was pushed into the path of an oncoming vehicle, then later, after we took care of Greta, someone took a couple of shots at us. All of these incidents have been reported to my superior, Master Sergeant Doug Hanover."

Westley James scowled. "I can't believe someone poisoned Greta," he said finally. He pinned Sean with a stern glare. "I need you to find the person responsible for all of this, understand?"

"Yes, sir. Believe me, I want to find the person who did this more than anyone."

"Staff Sergeant Morris was injured by the shooter." Jacey spoke up.

Westley's brows leveled upward. "You're okay?"

"Yes, sir. Just a flesh wound." Sean hesitated, then asked, "I'd like to speak to the staff who were working in the evening hours of the training center yesterday."

"Understood. Aiden Gomez was on duty, along with a few others assigned to shut down the kennel for the night. I'd start with him."

"Do you have a log of everyone who was here last evening?"

"Yes." Westley opened a file folder and removed a sheet of paper, then handed it to Sean.

"Aiden loves dogs," Jacey said. "He'd never do anything to harm them."

"I just want to see if he noticed anything unusual last night, that's all." That much was true, but Sean also knew that at this point in the investigation everyone was a suspect.

Even Jacey.

Not that he really believed she would harm her own K-9 partner, but he couldn't afford to overlook any remote possibility.

Getting personally involved is exactly what had gotten him into trouble with Liz Graber. Thinking her ex-husband had gotten the message, he'd asked Liz out on a date. The night they'd dined at a local restaurant off base, Liz's ex had followed them, and then he'd killed her. If Sean hadn't asked Liz out on a personal level, she never would have died that night.

No way was he going down that path again.

"Staff Sergeant Morris?"

He snapped his head up to find Westley James staring at him impatiently. "Yes, sir?"

"When would you like to speak to Aiden Gomez? He's here in the morning for four-and-a-half hours, then again in the late evening for three hours."

"If he's here, I'd like to see him now, if that's okay."

Westley nodded. "Very well. You can use the empty trainer office at the end of the hall. It's next to Jacey's."

"Thank you, sir."

Westley reached for his phone and gave a curt order for Airman Gomez to report to the office on the double.

"This way," Jacey said, leading him down the hall to the empty office. She opened the door, then hovered in the doorway for a moment. "I'm going to spend a few hours working with a group of puppies, so there's no need for you to hang around after you're finished with Aiden."

"I see." Despite his internal promise to keep his distance, he was disappointed. "Will you do me a favor?"

She eyed him warily. "Like what?"

"Call me when you're ready to leave. It's not safe for you to be alone, Jacey. I plan to sign out a vehicle, so there will be no need to take taxis back and forth."

She pursed her lips, then nodded. "Okay."

He let out a silent breath of relief. "Thanks."

Jacey looked as if she wanted to say something more,

but then she glanced down the hall and smiled. "Hi, Aiden. How are you?"

"Not good—I just heard about Greta." The young airman was visibly upset. "I saw she wasn't in her kennel, but I didn't realize she was sick. What happened?"

"We don't know for sure but we think she was given something that made her sick," Jacey said, and Sean was glad that she'd glossed over the cause of Greta's illness. "That's what Staff Sergeant Morris wants to talk to you about."

"Come in, Aiden." Sean gestured the young man to step forward. "What time did you work last night?"

"From nineteen hundred to twenty-two thirty." Aiden glanced back at Jacey. "Greta was fine in her kennel when I left."

"I believe you," Jacey said.

"Aiden, I need to know if you saw anything unusual around any of the kennels. Any liquids or substances that aren't normally around."

Aiden frowned. "No, sir, I didn't. We have very strict rules here because it's our job to make sure the dogs are safe."

"Okay, then, what about people?" Sean pressed. "Did you see anyone around who you normally don't see that late at night?"

Aiden's gaze turned thoughtful. "I did see someone wearing the usual battle dress uniform, but he or she had the collar turned up to hide their face, and had a hat on, so I didn't see who it was. The person was slender—made me think it was a woman, but I can't honestly say for sure."

Sean's pulse kicked up a beat and he pulled out the log, then glanced at Jacey. "Looks like both Misty Walsh and Reba Pokorny are on the log, although Misty left before twenty hundred." He found it telling that Jacey's name was not on the list, which proved it wasn't foolproof.

"Misty is a trainer, and Reba is a caretaker, like Aiden," Jacey said. "To be honest, it wouldn't be that difficult for someone to slip past without signing the log."

"You think the person I saw gave something to Greta that harmed her?" Aiden asked, his expression horrified. "I can't believe Misty or Reba would do something like that. Especially Reba."

Sean wondered if Aiden had a thing for Reba. "We don't know that for certain, so don't go around saying that, okay? It could be that the person you saw may have witnessed something, just like you did."

Aiden's expression cleared, and he nodded. "I understand. Everyone is considered innocent until proven guilty."

That was true in a court of law, but in police work, Sean tended to view it the other way around. Everyone was a suspect until cleared by either an alibi or evidence to the contrary.

And the glimpse Aiden had gotten of a person hiding behind a turned-up collar and hat was his first clue.

He only wished there was more to go on than a vague description that could include just about anyone.

FIVE

Jacey spent a couple of hours working with Aiden and three of four puppies that he'd helped to foster a few months ago. The mother had defended her pups against a coyote and, despite her serious injuries, had thankfully recovered. Aiden had named the four puppies after national parks; the two females were Shenandoah and Denali, the two males Smoky and Bryce. Shenandoah was the runt of the litter and hadn't taken well to training, so Aiden had been allowed to keep her as his own.

The other three pups were K-9 stars in the making.

"Good job, Aiden," she said when the three pups followed each of his commands. "You really have a great rapport with those pups. They respond to you very well."

"Thanks." Aiden ducked his head in embarrassment, but smiled at the praise. "I love working with them. I can't thank you enough for agreeing to teach me how to train them."

"My pleasure." She yawned and had to force her eyes to remain open. Every muscle in her body ached from the combination of hitting the asphalt and lack of sleep.

"You look tired," Aiden said with a frown. "Maybe you should try to get some rest."

She wanted nothing more, but couldn't leave the training center without calling Sean. And she wanted to head over to the clinic to check on Greta. "Soon," she promised.

Honoring her word, she called Sean. He answered almost immediately. "Jacey? Everything okay?"

She yawned again. "Uh, yeah. Other than being exhausted. Listen, I'd like to head over to see Greta at the kennel before heading back to take a nap. Do you want to meet me at the veterinary clinic?"

"No, I'll pick you up there. I have a hard-top jeep from the motor pool. I'll be there in ten minutes."

She was too tired to argue. "Okay."

Sean arrived within his allotted time frame, and she gratefully climbed into the passenger seat. Even walking the short distance to the clinic seemed an overwhelming task.

"Thanks," Jacey said when Sean came over to open her door for her. "Why don't you look as tired as I feel?"

"I completed my reports, then slept for a couple of hours this morning." Sean held open the veterinary-clinic door for her, too. "I need to drive Greta's blood sample to the state lab when we're finished here."

She'd forgotten about that, but knowing that Sean would personally deliver the sample was reassuring. "Good morning," she greeted the airman behind the desk. "I'd like to talk to Captain Roark and see my K-9 partner, Greta."

"One moment, please." The airman left, returning a few minutes later. "Dr. Roark will see you in exam room number four."

"Thanks." Jacey led the way into the exam room and dropped into the visitor chair, resting her head back against the wall. "I'm not sure having a few hours of sleep is enough to make a long drive," she said to Sean. "Maybe you should wait until morning."

"I'll be all right," he said. "I'm used to working long hours with little sleep."

She and Greta had done the same overseas, but apparently she'd grown soft while being back at Canyon.

The back door opened and Dr. Roark came in leading Greta by an office leash. Jacey's K-9 responded instantly to her presence and when Dr. Roark picked up the dog and set her on the stainless-steel surface, Jacey wrapped her arms around Greta's neck and buried her face in the animal's soft fur.

"It's so good to see you, Greta." Jacey lifted her head and smiled as the dog licked her face and thumped her tail on the table. Jacey lifted her gaze to Dr. Roark. "She looks so much better."

Dr. Roark nodded. "She's responded exceptionally well to the fluids I've given her." He gestured to the small bump beneath the fur on the animal's neck. "This is almost completely gone. See? We place the fluid under the skin and it slowly gets absorbed into her bloodstream. I think another small bolus will do the trick."

Relieved, she scratched Greta carefully between her ears. "I can't wait to bring her home."

"Actually, if you're willing to sit here for another hour, I think you can." Dr. Roark glanced at his watch. "I need to draw another blood sample to check her kidney function. If the numbers continue to improve the way they have been, then I can give another fluid bolus and release her into your care."

"Really?" The wave of relief pushed past her exhaustion. "Then I'll wait."

"We both will," Sean corrected.

Dr. Roark nodded and gestured to the two visitor

chairs. "Make yourself at home. I'll take Greta back and get going on the blood work."

Jacey gave Greta one last kiss and stepped back so Dr. Roark could take her back. She sank into the chair and once again rested her head against the wall.

Sean dropped into the seat beside her. "I'm glad Greta is better."

"Me, too." She yawned again and closed her eyes. Maybe she'd just rest for a minute.

The next thing Jacey knew, Sean was softly calling her name. "Jacey? Wake up—Dr. Roark has Greta ready for you."

"Huh?" She lifted her head from Sean's shoulder and rubbed her eyes. Embarrassed at how she had used Sean as a pillow, she turned her attention to Greta, who was standing near her chair. "Hey, girl. Ready to go?"

Greta wagged her tail and licked Jacey's hand. There was a large bubble beneath Greta's fur from the second fluid bolus, so Jacey made sure to avoid that area as she gave Greta's coat a good rub.

Then she took Greta and patted Sean's arm. "Friend, Greta. Friend."

Greta sniffed him long and hard before wagging her tail.

"You'll need to take her outside frequently," Dr. Roark warned. "The more fluid she absorbs, the more she'll have to go."

"I understand." Jacey didn't care how much work was involved as long as she was able to take Greta with her. "Thank you for everything."

"You're welcome." Dr. Roark handed over the office leash and then provided a small square box containing Greta's blood sample to Sean. "I expect a copy of the results when they're ready."

"I will," Sean promised. They left the exam room. "I'm parked around the corner, so you and Greta should wait here in the lobby."

"I think we should stick together," Jacey countered. "All three of us have been under attack by whoever is behind this."

Sean's expression turned serious. "Yeah, you might be right about that."

They kept Greta between them as they left the clinic. The streets were busy at noontime with airmen and officers going out for lunch and doing Christmas shopping at the BX. The Christmas lights weren't as bright during the daytime, but wreaths decorated each lamppost providing a cheery atmosphere.

The drive to their temporary home didn't take long. Jacey walked around the back side of the property, which wasn't visible from the road, and allowed Greta to do her business. Sean watched over her and, when they were done, unlocked the door for her and Greta.

Inside, she took Greta around the house, familiarizing the K-9 with their temporary living arrangements. The place was only sparsely furnished, but she was pleasantly surprised to find a six-foot fake Christmas tree in the corner of the room, with a Nativity scene spread out beneath it. Greta sniffed at everything cautiously, then went over to drink water from a stainless-steel bowl Jacey had set next to her food dish in the kitchen.

"They must have left in a hurry to leave the Christmas tree and Nativity scene behind," Jacey said.

"I guess so." He watched Greta drinking from the water dish. "You seem to have covered everything."

"Yes, even Greta's vest for when she needs to get back to work." She yawned again. "I'll stretch out on the sofa for a while in case Greta needs to go out again."

"I hope to be back in a couple of hours," Sean said as he walked to the door. He glanced back with a frown. "I'd feel better about leaving if you were armed."

"Greta will watch over me."

Sean hesitated, then nodded. "Okay. See you later."

After he left, she locked the door and turned on some Christmas music for background noise, before stretching out on the sofa with Greta at her side. She thought she'd fall asleep instantly but found herself worrying about Sean driving all the way to the San Antonio crime lab on his own. Granted, no one other than his boss knew that he was driving a jeep, but still...

If not for Greta needing close monitoring, and frequent trips outside, she would have insisted on going along. Before drifting off to sleep, Jacey prayed that God would watch over Sean.

Bringing him back, safe and sound.

Sean kept a keen eye on the traffic behind him as he left Canyon. He hadn't signed the jeep out under his name, but had used his boss's instead and kept the paperwork out of the official file. Yet, that didn't mean he was willing to let down his guard.

The trip to San Antonio didn't take quite as long as he'd expected. He handed over Greta's blood sample, then turned and headed straight back to base. He had taken his computer with him and planned to continue working the investigation from their temporary living quarters.

He'd gotten photos of both female training-center employees who were on duty last evening and had interviewed them both over the phone. Of course, both women denied having anything to do with Greta. Next, he decided to dig into their backgrounds, see if there were any red flags there. He'd also left a message with Staff Sergeant Cronin about what they'd found at the parking lot.

Jacey was still asleep on the sofa when he returned to the house. Greta met him at the door and he held out his hand, hoping she remembered him from the clinic. He needn't have worried; Greta was a smart dog and didn't hesitate to press her nose against him.

He took Greta out into the backyard for a moment, sweeping his gaze over the area. But he didn't see anyone, not even a curious face from a neighbor's window.

When he returned inside, he set up his laptop on the kitchen table, keeping his phone on Vibrate so as not to disturb Jacey.

If Cronin didn't call him back within the hour, he'd have to try him again. Granted, the guy had worked the night shift, but Sean had to believe they'd found some sort of evidence at the parking lot.

He pulled up the background he'd started on Reba Pokorny, but she was a relatively new airman, transferred over from basic training just four months ago.

Too new to get into trouble? Maybe.

He was about to switch gears and begin looking at Misty Walsh when his phone rumbled against the tabletop. He swept up his phone, grimacing as he realized Jacey had woken up and was peering at him sleepily over the back of the sofa.

"Staff Sergeant Morris," he answered.

"This is Staff Sergeant Cronin, returning your call."

"Thank you. I'm interested in what evidence you were able to recover from the parking lot."

Cronin sighed. "Nothing."

Sean frowned. "What do you mean, *nothing*? Two shots were fired—there has to be something the gunman left behind."

"We waited for daylight and didn't find a single iota of evidence," Staff Sergeant Cronin said in a curt voice. "If not for the wound on your arm, I'd wonder if you didn't make the whole story up."

Sean's gaze met Jacey's, his chest tightening as he realized this was how she'd been treated by the Special Forces after reporting her incidents. It was awful to have someone in authority believing you lied about something so serious.

"There has to be something," Sean insisted. "The bullet that grazed my arm has to be there somewhere."

There was a long pause. "I guess we can try again," Staff Sergeant Cronin said without enthusiasm.

"We can use Greta," Jacey whispered from her spot on the sofa. "She has an incredible nose for gunpowder."

Sean nodded. At this point, he trusted Greta's nose more than the less-than-ambitious Staff Sergeant Cronin.

"Never mind," he told Cronin. "I have a better idea."

"Suit yourself." Cronin obviously didn't think Sean was going to find anything they'd missed.

"I will. Thanks for the call." He disconnected and set his phone aside. He supposed there was a remote chance the shooter had returned to the area and found the bullets on his own, but Sean didn't think so.

A smart gunman would have picked up the spent shell casings, then disappeared from sight. Returning to the scene of a crime was something to avoid at all costs.

Then again, some criminals weren't smart. That was exactly how the cops were able to catch them.

"Sean?"

He glanced up at Jacey's soft, questioning tone. "Yeah?"

"What do you think of giving Greta's nose a try?"

"I like it, if you think she's up to the task."

"Come, Greta." The dog instantly went to Jacey's side. "Sit."

The dog sat and stared up at Jacey with adoration.

"She seems fine," Jacey said. "It looks like most of her fluid bolus has been absorbed. I say we give her a chance and see how it goes. If she gets tired, we can always stop."

He wasn't about to argue. "I'm in. Let's go."

"Give me a few minutes." Jacey disappeared into one of the bedrooms, returning with Greta's vest. She strapped it over Greta's back and the dog straightened, looking as if she was on full alert.

"Amazing," he murmured. "She knows it's time to work."

"Yes, she does." Jacey gave Greta a small treat, then clipped on her leash. "We're ready when you are."

He slipped on his jacket as Jacey donned hers. Together they headed outside to where he'd left the jeep parked in the driveway. The south parking lot wasn't far, and he pulled into a slot on the opposite side from where the incident had taken place.

Jacey let Greta out the back, and the dog stood alert at her side. "You thought the shot came from the northeast, correct?"

"Yeah, but we shouldn't limit ourselves to just that area." He cast his gaze about the parking lot. "This way. Let's start where we were standing when we heard the shots."

They covered the distance, roughly thirty yards, and took the same position. Jacey was to his left and he'd been standing on the right. The shot had grazed his right biceps from behind.

Wait a minute. He turned in a circle until he was once again facing the direction they'd been headed last night. "We need to check the southwest, too."

"That's closer to the south gate, where two airmen are stationed 24/7," Jacey pointed out.

"I know—that's why I thought the shot came from behind. But I honestly can't say for sure, now in the light of day, so we need to check them both."

"Okay." Jacey bent toward Greta and held out a bullet for the dog to sniff. "Find," she commanded, releasing the leash.

Greta lowered her nose and began to sniff the ground, making circular patterns as she moved around the parking lot. Jacey followed close at her side, not saying much other than occasionally offering encouragement.

He was beginning to think their attempts to find evidence would be futile when Greta disappeared into some brush straight ahead of the spot where they'd started.

"Sean!" Jacey's voice held a note of excitement. "Greta found something!"

"What?" He jogged over to where the dog sat at attention. Nestled in the dirt was a brass shell casing. Only it wasn't a spent one, ejected after the bullet had been fired, but a full one.

"I don't believe it," he muttered, pulling an evidence bag from his pocket and using it to pick up the shell. "I can't believe the shooter actually dropped a bullet."

"I know, right? I think there must have been spent casings here, too, because Greta alerted in several other spots. But this was the only find." She hesitated, then added, "Look at this black spot here. I think it may be from a stubbed-out cigarette."

"Hmm." Sean rose to his feet. "This is evidence that someone was here, but it doesn't help our case. Anyone on base could have dropped a bullet and smoked a cigarette. We need to find the actual slugs that were used."

"We'll keep looking. Now that we believe the shooter

may have stood here, we have a better idea where to look for bullet fragments." Jacey placed Greta back on leash and they returned to their initial location.

This time, Jacey faced Greta toward the area opposite from where the shooter may have been. Where there was a good chance the bullet may have landed. She repeated her command to find, and Greta went to work.

Again, he thought their efforts would be fruitless, when suddenly Greta once again disappeared into the brush. "Sean! She found one!"

He crossed the lot and peered over Jacey's shoulder. A somewhat mashed slug was lying in the brush. The fact that it was misshapen convinced him this was the one that had creased his arm. The one that had missed them completely could be in Timbuktu for all he knew.

"Greta, you're incredible," he said as he pulled out another evidence bag. He picked up the slug and tucked it next to the unspent shell. He looked at Jacey. "This is exactly what we needed."

"I'm glad." Her smile was hesitant, and he was once again struck by a wave of awareness. Before he could talk himself out of it, he caught her close in a warm hug.

She stiffened for a fraction of a second before wrapping her arms around his waist and returning his embrace.

Holding Jacey in his arms felt right, but it didn't take long for him to remember his secret promise to keep his distance. He loosened his grip and took a subtle step back, trying to force her cranberry-vanilla from overwhelming him.

He couldn't fail Jacey the same way he'd failed Liz.

Not just for her sake, but his own.

Because if anything happened to Jacey, he'd never get over it.

SIX

Bending over, Jacey rubbed Greta's glossy coat in an attempt to hide her reaction to Sean's embrace. She liked being held in his arms, more than she should.

For a split second she'd remembered being roughly and painfully grabbed by Lieutenant Colonel Turks, but quickly shoved the memory away. Instead, she welcomed Sean's strong arms cradling her close. The woodsy scent of his aftershave had provided a calming effect, until he'd abruptly pulled away, leaving her feeling empty, lonely and confused.

Logically, she knew he only saw her as an old high school friend, nothing more. And she wasn't interested in a relationship, either. Which was why she absolutely needed to keep her heart protected from the lethal impact of Sean's good looks and charm.

"Good girl," she murmured to Greta. "Even after being sick, you performed like a trooper."

"I'll drop you off at the house before handing over this evidence," Sean said. "Greta deserves some rest."

"That she does," Jacey agreed. She straightened and looked at Sean. "If you want my opinion, the bullet fragment and the shell should go directly to the state lab. I wish there was a way to prove the shooter had smoked a cigarette there, too."

He nodded thoughtfully. "I agree on both counts. It was clear from my conversation with Staff Sergeant Cronin that he wasn't very interested in finding this evidence."

"Oh, Sean." Jacey's heart squeezed in her chest. "I'm afraid that's my fault. I'm persona non grata within the Special Forces because of my allegation against Turks and now that you're stuck with me, the stink is rubbing off on you. I'd completely understand if you want to distance yourself from me."

"Not a chance," Sean responded without hesitation. "There's something going on here, and any Special Forces cop that doesn't do their best to get answers doesn't deserve to wear the uniform."

She appreciated his stout loyalty, but couldn't help thinking that he had no idea what he was facing. She shook off the deep sense of foreboding and walked over to the jeep. Greta kept pace at her side, and Jacey was impressed at how well her K-9 had performed today.

"In you go, girl." She opened the back of the jeep and Greta gracefully jumped inside. After shutting the door behind her, Jacey went to the passenger-side door and slid in.

Sean didn't say much as he drove back to the house. Her nap had helped a bit, but she still had a nagging headache and was famished.

She glanced at Sean. "Do you think we could pick up something to eat at Carmen's?"

He flashed a wry grin. "You read my mind. I'm starving. Besides, it's too late for another drive to the San Antonio crime lab. I'll take the evidence in tomorrow."

Carmen's was an Italian restaurant on base with carryout service. Sean ordered a large spinach-and-eggplant lasagna to go.

"Here, I'll pay my share," Jacey said, digging money out of the pocket of her uniform.

"No way. This Branson Bulldog isn't going to make a fellow Branson Bulldog pay for a meal."

She rolled her eyes at his lame joke. Their old high school days seemed a long time ago, although she still remembered how cute Sean had been wearing his bulldog letterman jacket. He'd been a track star, and she'd loved watching him race.

He handed the white paper bag with their carryout order to her. The spicy scent of tomato sauce, oregano and cheese filled the interior of the jeep. Jacey noticed that he kept a close eye on the rearview mirror as he took a long winding path back to their temporary living quarters.

Jacey took Greta out back for a few minutes and when she returned to the kitchen Sean had the table set with the lasagna in the center. He'd gotten salads to go, as well, a small bowl at each place setting.

"Looks and smells delicious," she said as she filled Greta's food and water dishes. After washing her hands, she joined Sean at the table. Glancing at him beneath her lashes, she clasped her hands together and bowed her head. "Heavenly Father, please bless this food we are about to eat. Thank You for healing Greta so quickly and please continue to guide us on Your chosen path, amen."

"Amen," Sean murmured.

She was pleased that he'd joined her in prayer. He scooped out lasagna for her, then for himself.

"Thanks." She sampled the lasagna and wasn't disappointed. "Amazing."

Sean nodded, too busy eating to answer. She watched him for a moment, tempted to pinch herself to prove they were sitting here, sharing a meal after ten years had passed since they'd last seen each other. She felt bad about the way his fellow Special Forces cops were treating him but, at the same time, couldn't deny that God had brought them together for a reason.

She only hoped and prayed that they'd find out who was behind these attacks in time to salvage their reputations.

And before anyone else got hurt.

"This hits the spot," Sean said, breaking the silence. "My gram loves spinach-and-eggplant lasagna. I bring it out to her at least once a month."

She glanced at him in surprise. "I didn't realize your grandmother was living in the area."

"I moved her here two years ago. She was lonely back in Branson, Missouri, and I couldn't get out there to see her as often as I wanted. Having her in a small house close by enables me to visit on a weekly basis."

She was touched by the way he cared for his grandmother. "Is she your maternal grandmother?"

A shadow crossed his blue eyes. "Yes. I didn't know my father and didn't maintain contact with my stepfather's family."

She could hear the tension in his tone when he mentioned his stepfather and wondered what their relationship was like. Her parents had passed away several years go in a horrible traffic accident, leaving her and Jake alone. They'd always been close, but losing their parents had bound them together even closer.

After Jake had died, she'd felt adrift, unable to find her own place in the world.

Reuniting with Sean had changed that. There was a connection between them, and not just because of their shared past, but because they shared the same values.

The way he'd prayed with her at meals and his overall sense of decency. Not to mention the way he'd believed in her when no one else had. Her smile was wistful. "I'd love to meet your grandmother sometime."

Sean appeared startled at her comment, then quickly recovered. "Of course. Gram would love that." He ate the last bit of lasagna on his plate, then sat back with a sigh. "I'm stuffed."

She smiled, stood and stacked their dirty dishes together. "Me, too."

"I'll help," Sean protested.

"Washing dishes isn't women's work?" she teased.

"No, ma'am. Gram would flay me with the sharp end of her tongue if she heard me say anything like that." He carried the half-empty lasagna pan to the counter and covered it before placing it in the fridge. "My grandmother was an old army nurse. She didn't take attitude from anyone."

"That's amazing. Was your mother a nurse, too?" She filled one side of the sink with sudsy water.

"Yes, but she didn't keep working after getting married to my stepfather." The shadow was back in his gaze. "He insisted she stay home."

She glanced at him. "I get the impression you and your stepfather don't get along."

"We don't." Sean's voice was flat and hard. "I haven't seen him in ages and heard he passed away last year."

"I'm sorry." She'd obviously poked at a festering wound.

He blew out a breath and picked up a dish towel. "It's not your fault. He's just not a pleasant subject."

They finished washing and drying their dinner dishes in silence. She wanted to ask why Sean and his stepfather didn't get along, but could tell by the hard set to his jaw that he wasn't about to open up about his past.

Thinking back to their time at high school, she realized that Sean had come to their house often, but Jake hadn't gone to Sean's at all.

Had Sean been ashamed of his stepfather? She didn't know and couldn't ask Jake, either.

Sean alone was the only one who could answer her questions. And that wasn't an option at the moment.

As she dried her hands on a towel, her phone buzzed. She pulled it out, frowning at the unfamiliar number. Hesitantly, she answered, "Senior Airman Burke."

"This is Staff Sergeant Misty Walsh. I hope you don't mind me bothering you, but I was wondering if you'd have some time to talk. Privately."

Jacey's gaze clashed with Sean's and she covered her phone with her hand. "This is Misty Walsh," she whispered. Removing her hand, she added, "Yes, of course I'll talk to you, Misty. Do you have time tonight?"

"No, not tonight." Misty's response was swift and Jacey imagined she was hiding somewhere while making this call. "Tomorrow. In the daylight. Off base."

"Off base works for me. What time?" Jacey's heart thudded with anticipation and she kept her gaze locked on Sean's. "And where?"

"There's a coffee shop known as the Cozy Coffee Café, about six miles off base heading toward San Antonio. I'll meet you there at ten hundred hours."

"Ten at the Cozy Coffee Café," she repeated. "We'll be there."

"Wait, who's we?" Misty's voice rose with agitation. "Come alone or don't come at all."

"I meant me and my K-9, Greta," Jacey hastened to reassure her. "Misty, can you tell me what this is about?"

"You know." Her tone was full of bitterness. "Lieutenant Colonel Turks."

Jacey sucked in a harsh breath. "You've had experience with him, too?"

"Tomorrow, ten sharp." Misty disconnected from the line without saying anything further.

Jacey set her phone aside, trying to suppress a shiver. "I don't think Misty is the one who harmed Greta," she told Sean. "Seems as if she wants to talk to me about the lieutenant colonel."

"You're not going alone," Sean said in a tone that brooked no argument. "It's too dangerous."

She nodded, her mind swirling. "I know. You can sit in the back of the cafe to keep an eye on things. I'll have Greta with me, too."

"I hope it's not a trap," Sean muttered.

"It won't be." Jacey could hardly believe that Misty Walsh was another of Lieutenant Colonel Turk's victims.

Where there were two, there had to be more. Maybe if they all banded together, they could bring charges against the powerful commander.

They all couldn't be viewed as *not credible*, could they?

After Jacey and Greta disappeared into the bedroom to get some sleep, he stayed up at the kitchen table, combing through Misty Walsh's background.

It wasn't difficult to confirm she'd been deployed to Kabul, Afghanistan, under Lieutenant Colonel Turk's ultimate command. Sean stared at the roster, grimly wondering how many female airmen this guy assaulted.

And how many more might be next if they didn't find a way to bring him to justice.

Jacey had been one of the brave few who'd tried, and

while her initial attempt may have failed, he was convinced she'd ultimately succeed.

The attacks on Jacey and Greta and the gunshots fired at the parking lot had to be related to her allegations against the lieutenant colonel. Nothing else made sense.

All he had to do was to figure out who on base might be doing the deed on the colonel's behalf.

Exhaustion finally caught up with him, so he stretched out on the sofa and allowed sleep to claim him.

The following morning, he woke up stiff and sore from sleeping on the sofa, but feeling better having gotten a solid nine hours of sleep. He stretched and padded into the kitchen to start coffee. He frowned, unable to remember if Jacey drank coffee or not. Just to be safe, he filled a red tea kettle and put it on the stove.

He'd brought a carton of eggs over from his place, so once the coffee was brewed, he proceeded to cook breakfast. Jacey joined him a few minutes later. "Morning," she said briefly before taking Greta outside into the backyard.

The teakettle whistled and he turned off the flame beneath the burner. He watched through the window at the sink, admiring how pretty Jacey was, even first thing in the morning. It was too easy to remember how well she'd fit into his arms yesterday, and how difficult it had been to let her go.

Jacey and Greta returned a few minutes later. "Coffee smells great."

"Help yourself. The scrambled eggs are just about ready if you're interested."

"No complaints from me." Jacey gestured toward the teapot. "You drink tea?"

"No, but I wasn't sure if you did." He felt his cheeks flush with embarrassment. "Anyway, I thought we'd drive to the San Antonio crime lab to drop off the bullets prior to heading over to the Cozy Coffee Café."

"Sounds good." She dropped into a chair and cradled her coffee mug. "I can't believe Misty reached out to me. I wonder why she waited so long?"

"Good question. You've been back on base since October, right?"

"Yeah." She took a sip of her coffee. "Maybe I was wrong about Misty being involved in what happened to Greta. What better way to throw off suspicion than to attempt to form an alliance?"

He piled eggs on her plate along with toast and handed it to her. "You're starting to think like a cop."

Her lips quirked in a smile. "Comes from hanging around one."

"Or from having good instincts." He returned to the table with his eggs, then waited to see if she wanted to pray again. Sean had drifted away from his faith after Liz Graber had been killed by her ex-husband right under his nose.

But he couldn't deny liking the way Jacey had prayed before dinner last night.

She clasped her hands together and bowed her head. He followed suit. "Dear Lord, we thank You for this food we are about to eat. And we ask that You keep us safe in Your care as we start our day, amen."

"Amen," he echoed.

Jacey glanced at him, thoughtfully. "I don't remember seeing you at church services."

He inwardly winced. "No, probably not."

She looked a little disappointed, but then smiled. "You should see how beautiful the church is decorated for Christmas. It's the best way to get into the holiday spirit."

He reluctantly nodded. "Maybe I should."

She didn't push, but sampled her eggs. "Yum. Delicious."

"You seem to enjoy whatever edible items are placed in front of you," he teased.

She flashed a saucy grin. "I love any and all food I don't have to cook."

That made him laugh. When they finished breakfast, they worked together to clean up the mess, and he couldn't help thinking about how comfortable he was around Jacey.

So much so that he'd almost told her about his stepfather's physical abuse. Something he'd never told anyone, not even her brother, Jake.

She'd backed off, so he let it go. Besides, he didn't want or need her sympathy. Old history was best kept in the past as far as he was concerned.

An hour later, after they'd both showered and changed, they were on the road in his recently acquired jeep. As always, he kept a careful eye out for any hint of a tail, but so far, he hadn't seen anything suspicious.

The drive to San Antonio didn't take long, and they arrived at the Cozy Coffee Café ahead of schedule. He purchased them both large coffees, then took a seat a couple of rows behind Jacey's table, where he was able to maintain a good view of the door, Jacey and the street outside the window.

Jacey also sat overlooking the road, ignoring the curious looks the barista behind the counter shot toward Greta. Jacey had pointed out the K-9's vest that identified her as a working dog, so the barista didn't say anything about the animal needing to leave.

The minutes ticked by slowly.

At one minute past ten, Jacey straightened in her seat. Sean immediately saw what captured her attention: a red-headed female was standing at the street corner on the opposite side of the road.

His pulse quickened, but he attempted to appear nonchalant. He stared down at the sports section of the newspaper in front of him without reading a word.

"No!" Jacey shouted, jumping to her feet at the same instant he heard a distinct thud. Sean abandoned his newspaper and followed Jacey outside.

A crowd of people were gathered around the prone figure lying at the side of the street. Misty's bright red hair was unmistakable in the sunlight.

"What happened?" Sean asked, wishing he'd ignored the stupid newspaper to keep an eye on Misty.

"A black pickup truck sideswiped her." Jacey and Sean pushed through the crowd to kneel beside Misty. "Did anyone call 911?"

"I did," a kid with baggy pants answered.

Sean felt for a pulse, slightly reassured to find a fast and thready beat. There was a long laceration on her scalp, blood coalescing on her pale skin. Her left arm was bent at an odd angle, clearly broken.

"Did you get a glimpse of the license plate?" he asked.

"No, the plate was liberally covered with mud." Jacey's dark gaze was full of guilt. "I believe the driver of the truck was the same person who shoved me into traffic, poisoned Greta and shot at us."

Sean couldn't disagree. This hit-and-run convinced him that Misty had information that would help Jacey's case against Lieutenant Colonel Ivan Turks.

Whoever had done this was willing to eliminate any and all potential witnesses.

Without caring about the consequences.

SEVEN

There was so much blood, covering Misty and pooling on the road beneath her. Fighting nausea, Jacey put her hand on Misty's uninjured arm. Overwhelmed with guilt and sorrow, Jacey couldn't get the image of the truck hitting Misty Walsh out of her mind; it played over and over again like a stuck loop.

"It's okay, Misty. Help is on the way." The trainer was unconscious, but that didn't stop Jacey from talking to her. The rise and fall of Misty's chest was reassuring, but Jacey knew head injuries could be tricky. Especially since Misty's was bleeding like crazy.

Greta sat beside Jacey, sniffing at the female airman as if there was something she could do to help.

"I hear the ambulance now." Sean's deep voice was oddly reassuring. He rose to his feet and scanned the crowd of gawkers. "Anyone see what happened?"

"A black truck ran the red light and hit her along the left side." The kid wearing saggy pants spoke up. "It was bad, man. Really bad."

Jacey found no comfort in the fact that the kid's story mirrored hers. As she stared down at Misty's pale features, she kept thinking that it should have been her lying there.

Who knew that they were planning to meet today? Misty had called Jacey's cell phone directly to make the arrangements.

Was it possible one or both of their phones had been bugged? She knew her cell number was on file with the air force and that anyone with access could look it up. Or had someone close to Misty overheard her making the call?

Jacey didn't like any of the possibilities.

The ambulance arrived and soon the EMTs had Misty bundled up on the gurney.

"Wait." Jacey stopped them with a hand on the EMT's arm. "Which hospital are you taking her to? She's a senior airman from Canyon Air Force Base."

The two EMTs looked at each other and shrugged. "It's the same distance either way. We'll take her to Canyon if that's what you'd prefer."

"I would." She stepped back and glanced at Sean. "I'd like to meet her at the hospital, too."

"It will take some time before we'll be able to see her," he cautioned.

"I know." Logically she knew this wasn't her fault; Misty had been the one to reach out to her, not the other way around, but this had all started with her allegation against Lieutenant Colonel Turks.

Maybe she should have just kept her mouth shut.

The minute the thought crossed her mind, she inwardly rejected it. No, what the lieutenant colonel did wasn't right. She was fortunate enough to have escaped, but what if others hadn't been able to?

What if Misty hadn't?

The man was a menace, using his power as a weapon against women. No one deserved to be assaulted. Women could contribute to keeping the country safe just as well as men did. Even if she ended up being forced to resign from the air force, she knew she wouldn't go back to change the fact that she'd pressed charges against Turks.

She needed to believe that someday justice would be served.

Greta sensed her inner turmoil and pressed her nose against Jacey's hand. Jacey rubbed the K-9 between the ears and then crossed over to Sean. "We need to get out of here."

"I know. This way."

They walked back to his jeep in silence, each lost in their thoughts. When they arrived at the hospital, Misty was still being cared for in the ER.

"I'm the Special Forces cop who was on the scene after the crash," Sean informed the triage nurse. "I need an update on Misty's condition."

"I'll get the doctor for you."

Five minutes later, a man wearing scrubs covered by a long white lab coat came out to the waiting area. "Staff Sergeant Morris?"

Sean and Jacey both stood and approached the captain. They saluted and then went at ease.

"I'm Captain Robertson," the doctor introduced himself. "I understand you were at the scene when this happened?"

"Yes, sir." Sean briefly described what Jacey and the other young man had seen. "I'd like to understand the extent of her injuries."

"Her left side took the brunt of the damage. She has a broken arm and leg. The arm has a significant compound fracture that will require surgery. She also has a collapsed lung on the left side that I was able to treat. I'm sure you noticed the laceration along the left side of her head."

"Has she woken up? Said anything?" Sean asked.

"No. She hasn't regained consciousness yet. I can have the nurse call you when she does."

"That would be great, thank you, sir." Sean handed the captain his contact information.

Awash in helplessness, Jacey watched the doctor walk away.

"There's nothing more we can do here," Sean said quietly.

"I know." That didn't mean she liked it. "Come, Greta." She followed Sean outside to the jeep. "Now what?"

"I'll keep digging for suspects."

Jacey put Greta in the back and then slid in beside Sean. As he headed back to the house, she considered their next options.

"We've assumed based on the log that the person Aiden saw in the kennel that night was female, but what if it wasn't? I think we need to broaden our search to men, and not just those employed by the training center."

"How would a man who didn't work there get access to Greta's kennel?"

She shook her head helplessly. "Steal it? Force someone to open it? Who knows? The fact is that we have to expand our pool of suspects."

"It's already a large pool, but I see what you're saying. I'll look into it—don't worry."

"We will." The stubborn glint was back in her eye. "I'm involved in this. After what happened to Misty…" She couldn't finish.

Sean pulled into the driveway and shut off the engine. He came around to open her door for her and for the second time in two days, she found herself cradled in his arms.

"She's strong. She'll pull through this," he murmured against her temple.

"I hope so." Her voice was muffled against his shirt and she breathed in his woody scent, then lifted her head to look up at him. "Thank you."

His brow levered up in surprise. "For what?"

"Being there for me." Keeping her gaze centered on his, she rose up on tiptoe and pressed her mouth against his.

He froze, and she feared he'd pull away, but he didn't. Instead he tugged her close and deepened their kiss. This was what she'd waited for. What she'd longed for. She reveled in his taste, the strength and warmth of his arms.

After several long moments, he finally lifted his head, breathing deep. "We can't do this. You're killing me, Jacey."

She couldn't help but smile. "Yeah? Well, after waiting ten years for you to kiss me, I figured it was time to take matters into my own hands."

His jaw dropped. "Ten years? You mean—"

"I've had a crush on you since high school." Seeing Misty lying on the gurney and hearing the extent of her injuries had convinced Jacey it was time to tell him the truth.

"I, uh, had no idea." He looked completely poleaxed by her declaration.

"I'm sure I was nothing more to you than Jake's annoying little sister," she teased. Greta poked her nose out from the back of the jeep, so she gestured for the dog to jump down.

He stared down at Jacey for a long moment. "Not exactly," he finally admitted. "I always thought you were pretty back then, but you're beautiful now."

"Really?" It was her turn to be caught off guard.

He nodded, then rubbed a hand along the back of his neck. "I— Things weren't good at home, so I pretty much stayed away from dating and friendships. Jake was the one guy I allowed myself to get close to, and even then, I never invited him to my house. I preferred hanging around yours, anyway."

"Because of your abusive stepfather?" she guessed.

His eyes widened in shock. "Yeah, but I didn't say he was abusive."

"You didn't have to. It was an easy assumption." She tilted her head to the side. "I'm sorry you had to go through that."

Sean let out a harsh laugh. "Me, too. But I finally convinced my mother to leave the jerk. But shortly thereafter, my mother was diagnosed with cancer and died within three months. After that, I joined the air force."

Her heart squeezed in her chest, and she placed a comforting hand on his arm. "I'm here if you want to talk."

"Thanks." His smile was strained. "But I think our time is better spent trying to figure out who is behind all of this."

She hesitated, then nodded. "All right. But just know, I'm here for you."

As they went inside, Jacey lightly touched her fingers to her still-tingling lips.

She didn't regret kissing Sean, but had the sense that he didn't feel the same way. His exact words were *we can't do this.*

Was it because of his abusive stepfather? Or something else?

Either way, Jacey was determined to get to the bottom of what was going through Sean's mind.

She'd planned to keep her distance, but that wasn't an option anymore. Certainly not after that toe-curling kiss.

They'd been given a second chance at a possible relationship.

If Sean had the courage to take it.

Kissing Jacey hadn't been part of his plan. But now that he'd tasted the sweetness of her lips, he wasn't sure he'd find the strength to stay away.

Remember Liz Graber, he harshly told himself. The image of how she looked lying dead on the floor was burned into his memory. Knowing that her ex-husband had taken the opportunity to kill her right under Sean's nose was a failure he'd have to live with for the rest of his life.

The only redeeming fact was that Sean had worked tirelessly to piece together the trace evidence needed to lock the guy up behind bars. At the time, he'd assumed he'd be demoted, but apparently bringing Liz's ex to justice had saved his reputation.

But it hadn't saved his heart.

And here he was, making the same mistake with Jacey. Getting too close and not keeping a professional distance.

If he was honest with himself, he'd say he'd already crossed the line by kissing her. Something he'd dreamed of doing ten years ago. And it rattled him to realize she'd felt the same way.

His emotions were tangled up in Jacey, no matter how hard he tried to unravel the hold she had on him.

Somehow, he had to keep his wits about him. No way was Jacey going to end up like Liz.

Not on his watch.

Jacey insisted on going to the training center for the afternoon, so he accompanied her and Greta, watching for a few moments as she put the animal through several training scenarios.

While Jacey worked with the K-9s, he did his best to stay focused on doing background checks of all the personnel on base who had even minor blemishes on their record in dealing with women. If the issue was Jacey's allegation against Turks, then someone must be holding a grudge against women who stand up for themselves against sexist behavior.

But there were so many, it was depressing. There were only two interesting items he'd uncovered. One was an allegation of inappropriate conduct against Bill Ullman, the cop who'd initially investigated Jacey's case, which had been filed just five months ago. The other was a formal assault complaint against his boss, Master Sergeant Hanover. The assault was two years ago, filed by a woman who Hanover had been dating. A lover's spat? Maybe. Regardless, he saved a copy of both incidents, although at this point, he was leaning toward Ullman as his primary suspect.

Then he switched gears to finish his report on the events of the morning. Less than ten minutes after he'd filed his report on Misty Walsh's hit-and-run, Master Sergeant Hanover called his cell phone.

"What's the connection between Senior Airman Walsh and Senior Airman Burke?" Hanover demanded.

"Misty asked Jacey if they could meet off base for coffee. She had something to tell her about Lieutenant Colonel Turks."

There was a long moment of silence. "You think she was assaulted, as well?" Hanover finally asked.

"We won't know for sure until she wakes up to tell us," Sean pointed out. It was interesting that his boss seemed very concerned about the assault. Maybe going through the issue with his former girlfriend had made him see how wrong he'd been to do such a thing. "But that's the working theory, yes."

"Hmm." Sean waited as his boss mulled over the information. "Do you believe her?"

"Jacey? Yes, I do."

Another long pause. "It's not easy going up against a lieutenant colonel without some hard evidence."

"No, sir. Yet it appears someone is trying to prevent us from doing just that."

"Be careful," Hanover said. "Oh, and be aware that Senior Airman Ullman isn't happy I transferred the case to you. I trust you to do a good job with it."

"Understood, sir." Maybe if Ullman had taken Jacey's concerns seriously, the airman would still have the case. Too bad for him.

Ullman had had at least one instance of attempted assault of a woman. Were there more that hadn't been reported? Sean felt as if he were walking through a maze blindfolded. The whole thing was beyond frustrating. Lieutenant Colonel Turks was halfway across the globe in Kabul, Afghanistan, while attempts were being made on military personnel here, at Canyon.

Sean needed a break in the case, and soon. Before anyone else was hurt, or worse.

He left the office Westley James had allowed him to use and crossed over to wait for Jacey. She and Greta joined him a few minutes later.

"You want me to pick up a pizza for dinner?" he asked.

"Sure." Her smile didn't reach her eyes. "Any news on Misty?"

"Not yet. We'll call the hospital for an update when we get home."

She nodded, her expression troubled. "Even if she

wakes up, there's no guarantee she'll remember anything about the driver of the truck that hit her."

"I know, but we still need to know what she wanted to discuss with you in the first place." It still bothered him that Misty had asked for Jacey to come alone.

Why exclude a cop?

Sean had more questions than answers.

Jacey gave Greta food and water, then called the hospital while he set the table. He set the pizza on the table, pleased that Jacey had requested the works, exactly the way he liked it.

Stop it, he told himself harshly. Focus on the case, not on the woman.

"Still not awake," Jacey said dejectedly as she dropped into the chair across from him. "But they think it's mostly because of her surgery. They had to place a rod and pins to align the bones in her left arm."

As horrible as it was, he knew it could have been much worse. He held out his hand, palm upward. "Let's pray for her."

She looked surprised by his suggestion but placed her hand in his and bowed her head. "Heavenly Father, we ask that You please heal Misty's injuries and help her wake up so we can seek justice against the person who did this to her. We also ask that You bless this food we are about to eat, and that You continue to guide us on Your chosen path, amen."

"Amen," he echoed.

She didn't remove her hand from his for a long moment. "I'm glad you suggested praying for Misty," she said, finally letting him go. "That was nice."

"Yeah." Truthfully, he'd surprised himself by making the request. Since reuniting with Jacey, he'd realized the importance of renewing his faith. "Maybe I should think about attending church services again, too. For more than just getting into the holiday spirit."

"That would be great." Jacey's smile was brighter than the lights on Christmas tree in the corner of the living room. "Have you ever spoken to Bill Ullman about the reports I made to him when the strange incidents started?"

He lifted a brow. "No, why?"

She shrugged and took another bite of her pizza. "I don't know, just curious."

"I figured there was nothing to gain by talking to him, since you mentioned he didn't take your concerns seriously. Although my boss did mention that he's not happy that I've been given the case." He didn't tell her what he'd found so far in the guy's file. One incident didn't make a murderer.

"That's interesting. Why would he care?" She lifted her head and stared out the window for a moment. Then her gaze narrowed and she abruptly leaped to her feet. "Sean! I think there's a fire over at the base-housing apartment complex."

"What?" He went over to see what she meant. Dusk was falling, but it was easy to see the dark cloud of smoke hovering over the building, obliterating the Christmas lights dangling from the light poles.

A coincidence? Not likely. Anyone looking at his personnel file or Jacey's would see that they both lived there.

Was this yet another attempt against them?

To silence one or both of them, for good?

EIGHT

"We need to head over there, see if they need help." Jacey bent over to fasten Greta's vest in place.

"We're not trained firefighters," Sean protested. "If this is an attempt to get to us, then we need to stay here where it's safe."

"You don't know that the fire is connected to us. Our military brothers and sisters need our help." Jacey secured a leash to Greta's vest. "I'm going to help them. They might need Greta's trained nose. You can stay here if you want."

"No way. You're not going alone." Sean's tone was clipped with anger. It occurred to her that this was the first time she'd seen him truly angry. "We'll take the jeep and if there is any evidence this is linked to us, we're out of there."

Parking would be a nightmare, but she decided to let it go.

The area around the apartment building was engulfed in chaos. For a moment, she wondered if Sean was right about this being a trap, but then she shook off the sliver of fear.

They needed to make sure everyone had gotten out of the building safely.

Greta sniffed at people as they passed by, and Jacey wondered if the perpetrator who'd started the fire used something that Greta could identify. The K-9 wouldn't pick up on scents like gasoline or fire-starter fluid, but if there was gunpowder or something similar, it was worth a shot.

This is what Greta trained for.

The firefighters were already on scene and not allowing any pedestrians to cross the perimeter. The scent of smoke was thick and heavy as the firefighters put out the blaze.

"Only the south building seems to be impacted," Sean murmured.

She nodded. "I noticed. They're soaking the north building with water to stop the fire from spreading, but it appears that they have it under control."

"I wonder where the fire originated?" Sean asked, staring at the third floor where it appeared the majority of the work was being done by the firefighters on scene.

Jacey shivered as the magnitude of the event washed over her. "My apartment is on the third floor."

Sean put his arm around her shoulders and gave her a quick squeeze. "Exactly."

The thought that this fire was set on purpose, maybe even in her unit, made Jacey feel sick. The person behind all of this obviously didn't care how many innocent people were hurt along the way.

Why had the perp set her apartment on fire while she wasn't there? To scare her?

Or was this all one big coincidence?

The fire chief turned to address the crowd of onlookers. "Has anyone seen Senior Airman Burke?"

Jacey swallowed hard and lifted her hand. "Here, sir."

He gestured for her to step forward, and she was re-

lieved that Sean stayed close at her side. They both saluted the senior officer. Greta was on full alert, her nose
sniffing constantly.

"Senior Airman Burke, your apartment has been
deemed the source of the fire." The fire chief's gaze
was stern. "Are you a smoker? Or did you leave candles
burning?"

"No, sir." Jacey tightened her grip on Greta's leash.
"I have never smoked. I don't have a real Christmas tree
or wreath and do not burn candles. I'm aware of what is
and isn't allowed on the premises, sir."

"Hmm." His stern expression softened. "Well, I'm
glad you weren't home when this happened. Thankfully, the sprinklers worked well and the fire was put
out quickly. Most of the damage was centered on your
apartment and those adjacent and beneath it. And most
of that is from water, not the fire itself."

Jacey sent up a quick prayer of thanks that no one was
injured as a result of the fire. But it still bothered her that
her apartment was used as the source of the blaze. "I'm
glad to hear that, sir."

"Has the fire been deemed arson?" Sean spoke up
for the first time. "I'm Staff Sergeant Morris, and I'm
investigating several previous attempts to harm Senior
Airman Burke. Hearing the source of the fire was her
apartment gives me a reason to believe this event is connected to the others."

"Not yet. Who is your superior officer?"

"I report directly to Master Sergeant Doug Hanover,
sir, but ultimately my CO is Captain Justin Blackwood."

"Fine." The fire chief nodded. "I'll let Captain Blackwood know when our investigation is complete. At this
point, all I can tell you is that it appears that the fire originated on the sofa."

Jacey opened her mouth to protest, but Sean nudged her and shook his head. This was the part of the military she didn't enjoy, when brass would only communicate among lines of authority.

It was her apartment that had been torched. Sean was the key cop investigating her case. The bureaucracy was beyond annoying.

"Dismissed," the fire chief said, turning away from them. Jacey had to grit her teeth together to prevent herself from saying something she'd regret. The last thing she needed was another negative note in her file.

The one currently sitting in there was bad enough.

"Come on." Sean tugged at her elbow. "Let's get out of here."

"Where are these airmen who can't return to their apartments going to sleep tonight?" Jacey asked as she allowed Sean to lead a weaving path through the crowd.

"I'm sure they'll be ordered to double up—they won't be stranded in the cold." Sean brushed aside her concern. "We need to get back to the house. I don't like being out in the open like this."

"No one would be crazy enough to make an attempt on us with all these people around." Even as she said the words, she realized that wasn't entirely true.

Misty had been struck by a truck in the bright light of day on a busy street with pedestrians milling about.

The person behind this was growing bolder. Jacey would be a fool to underestimate him or her.

Him. Deep down, she knew the person responsible was a man. Who else would care about her allegation against Lieutenant Colonel Turks? Even if a woman didn't quite believe her, it was unlikely that a female airman or officer would go to such lengths to silence her.

Not just her, but Misty, too.

The perp had to be a man. Someone with a lot to lose if the truth about the lieutenant colonel came to light.

But who?

The strong stench of cigarette smoke made her wrinkle her nose seconds before someone shoved past her. The person making their way through the crowd was wearing a uniform, complete with a cap, and had the collar turned up around the face.

"Wait! Sean! This way!" She jutted around another person, trying to follow the guy weaving through the crowd. There were so many people, all dressed similarly and wearing hats because of the cold December temperatures.

"What happened?" Sean asked, joining her. "Did you see someone?"

"I did, but he's gone now." She sighed and glanced around. "I'm sure it was the guy we're looking for."

"A guy?" Sean asked. "You saw his face?"

"Not exactly." She glanced around, battling a wave of dejection. So close. The perp had been so close! "But can you honestly come up with a reason why a woman would do this?"

"No, but that doesn't mean a woman isn't involved." Sean anchored his arm around her waist, providing a sense of safety and protectiveness. "It's not smart to rule anyone out, Jacey."

She didn't answer, but the image of Misty Walsh's pale, bloodstained face wouldn't go away.

Then she remembered the scent of cigarette smoke. "It's the same guy who shoved me from behind that first night. I know it. He reeked of the same stale cigarette smoke. As if he'd smoked an entire pack within the past few hours."

"Yeah, okay, but that doesn't exactly narrow down

our pool of suspects," Sean pointed out. "Almost half the personnel on base smoke."

He was right. She knew he was right.

But so was she. They were looking for a man who smoked and who didn't particularly like women. Or maybe liked them too much.

"Wait a minute." She stopped and looked at Sean. "Does Lieutenant Colonel Turks have family? Like a son?"

Sean shook his head. "That was the first thing I checked. He has a civilian ex-wife, and that's it. No other family listed on file."

"Does his ex-wife have kids?"

"No." She should have realized he'd check that, too, considering his experience with his own stepfather.

"Great." Her shoulders slumped with defeat. They were right back where they'd started two days ago.

No suspects, no way to narrow the list of airmen and officers living on base.

They were fresh out of clues.

Sean hustled Jacey through the crowd, looking over his shoulder at different time intervals to make sure they weren't followed.

He understood Jacey's frustration; in fact, he shared it. Just as they reached the playground located two blocks down from the apartment complex, a pretty blonde stepped in front of them. "I'm Heidi Jenks—I'd like to interview Senior Airman Burke about the fire that originated in her apartment."

"No comment," Sean said, holding up his hand so Jacey wouldn't respond.

"I was talking to Jacey Burke, not you," Heidi responded tartly. "I'm sure she can speak for herself."

Jacey didn't respond right away, as if weighing her options.

"Don't," Sean said in an undertone. "The last thing you need is to have your name splattered all over the base newspaper."

"Again, I think she can speak for herself," Heidi countered. "Jacey?"

"How did you know her first name?" Sean challenged, knowing there was no way to win the gender war.

Heidi looked taken aback. "I heard the fire chief mention her name."

"No, he only referred to her as Senior Airman Burke." Sean didn't like this one bit. "Not her first name. Which according to her file is listed as Jacelyn. So how do you know her nickname?"

"Okay, okay." Heidi lifted a hand in surrender. "If you must know, I learned about Jacey's allegation against the lieutenant colonel and thought it would be a good idea to do a story on it." She turned toward Jacey. "What do you think? Don't you want other women to be aware of what happened?"

"My allegation was deemed not credible," Jacey said in a low tone. "Why would you want to do a story on something that hasn't been validated?"

"Because I think it's important that all sides of the story are told and women need to be encouraged to stand their ground and fight back against this kind of thing," Heidi responded. "Do you really want the lieutenant colonel to have the last word?"

"Why does it matter, if no one believes me?" Jacey asked.

"Whoa, Jacey. You need to take some time to think about the ramifications of giving an interview." Sean didn't necessarily think that Heidi Jenks was up to something nefarious, but at the same time, he didn't want Jacey jumping into something she may regret later. The lieutenant colonel already had someone on base attacking her; why stir things up?

Heidi was focused on Jacey. "I don't want to rush you into anything, but I am interested in hearing your side of what happened. You're not the only woman on base who's had to deal with this. Here's my card. Give me a call when you feel like talking."

"Thanks." Jacey took the reporter's card and offered a wan smile.

"I look forward to hearing from you," Heidi said as she turned away.

"Wait!" Jacey took a few steps toward the reporter and Sean curled his fingers into fists to prevent himself from reaching for her.

"Change your mind already?" Heidi asked with a grin.

"No, but I do have a question for you. Do you know Misty Walsh?"

Sean didn't think he imagined the flash of recognition in the reporter's eyes.

"Why does it matter?" Heidi asked.

"Because she was seriously injured by a hit-and-run," Sean said.

Heidi's eyes widened with horror. "No! What happened?"

He was a little surprised she didn't know, but then remembered that the hit-and-run had taken place off base. None of this was Heidi Jenks's fault. He was letting his personal feelings toward Jacey run amok, viewing Heidi as an adversary rather than an ally.

"Someone driving a black truck ran a red light and hit her on the left side," Jacey answered. "She has a head injury, a broken arm requiring surgery and a broken leg, among other minor wounds. Now it's your turn to answer my question. Did you talk to Misty? Did she tell you about having an issue with the lieutenant colonel?"

Heidi nodded slowly. "Yes, she told me that I needed to dig into the issue of abuse among ranking officers, specifically Lieutenant Colonel Turks, and she specifically mentioned you." Her expression filled with concern. "Do you think that's why she was hit by the truck?"

"I do," Jacey said before Sean could interject another *no comment.* "Because she called to set up a meeting with me off base. She was hit before she reached the café."

"Oh, no," Heidi whispered. "How terrible."

"This is why it wouldn't be smart for Jacey to talk to you," Sean said firmly. "Maybe later, but not now."

"Sean's right," Jacey said, her brow furrowed. "Things are too dangerous. Misty's life is hanging in the balance as it is."

"I'm sorry," Heidi offered. "I had no idea."

"It's okay." Jacey flashed a weary smile. "It's not your fault, but I think it's best if you leave this alone for a while. Bad enough that some of us are in danger. I'd hate to see anything happen to you."

"I can take care of myself," Heidi said. "And my fiancé, Nick Donovan, won't let anything happen to me, either."

"Nick Donovan?" Jacey repeated. "I worked with him a bit while training Greta. He's an explosives expert and Greta is a bomb-sniffing K-9."

"Small world," Heidi said with a wry smile.

"Yes, well—" Jacey cleared her throat "—I'm hopeful the truth will come out sooner or later, and if it does, I promise to give you an exclusive."

Heidi's eyes lit up. "Thanks. Please let me know when you're willing to talk."

"I will," Jacey agreed. "Where are you headed? It's not smart for you to be alone."

"I'm meeting Nick at Carmen's," Heidi admitted. "And based on what you've just told me, it would be silly to turn down an escort."

Finally, a statement Sean could agree with. As he walked between the two women, Jacey keeping Greta close by, he found himself hoping that Heidi wouldn't end up in the crosshairs the way Jacey and Misty had been.

The person doing all of this had to make a mistake sooner or later. And Sean planned to be there when he or she did.

NINE

Jacey and Heidi chatted a bit while Sean drove them to Carmen's. He parked nearby, and the three of them with Greta headed to the restaurant. Nick must have been waiting for them, because he came outside to meet them. Jacey and Sean each gave a quick salute in deference to his rank of captain.

"Jacey, it's good to see you again," Nick said.

"You, too. Oh, and this is Staff Sergeant Sean Morris with Special Forces. Sean, this is Captain Nick Donovan."

Now that the formalities were over, the two men shook hands. "Nice to meet you, Captain," Scan said.

Nick nodded and glanced at Heidi. "You're late," he chided gently with a private smile. "Because of the fire?"

"Of course!" She leaned up to kiss him. "Thanks for being patient."

"Always," he murmured, his gaze full of love.

Jacey couldn't help but sigh at how adorable they were together.

"Captain, you may want to keep a close eye on your fiancée over the next few weeks." Sean's serious tone brought the cheerfulness down a notch. "She's investigating a story that has attracted danger."

"The fire?" Nick asked with a frown.

"Not just the fire, but about allegations of assault against a high-ranking officer," Jacey said. She knew Heidi would fill him in anyway. "The fire is just one of the attempts against me, among others."

"Heidi?" Nick put his arm around the petite blonde. "Is this true?"

"Yes," Heidi admitted. "I didn't realize that one of the women I spoke to yesterday, Misty Walsh, was involved in a hit-and-run crash earlier today, before Jacey and Misty could meet. They both have experience with a particular senior officer. That, combined with the fact that Jacey's apartment is the source of the fire, makes it doubly suspicious."

"No more rushing off to cover stories alone," Nick said in a grim tone. "I'll go with you from now on."

"Good plan," Sean said with a nod.

"Do you have a list of suspects?" Nick asked.

"I wish I did," Sean admitted. "But so far there's very little evidence. There are a few items up at the San Antonio crime lab, but so far I haven't heard anything."

"Let me know if you need help." Nick's expression was troubled.

"I will. Excuse me." Sean pulled his ringing phone from his pocket and moved away from the other couple. Jacey went with him, curious about who was calling. "Staff Sergeant Morris," he said by way of greeting.

Heidi and Nick disappeared into the restaurant as Jacey strained to hear the other side of the conversation.

"She is? Great, we'll be right there." Sean slid his phone back into his pocket. "Good news—Misty Walsh is conscious and able to talk."

"Thank You, Lord," Jacey whispered, knowing that God had answered their prayers. "That's wonderful. Can we go there now?"

"Absolutely. It's just a block away, so no sense taking the jeep, but stay close," Sean warned. "Keep Greta on your left, and I'll stay to the right."

Jacey wasn't going to argue.

Inside the hospital, the lobby was warm and brightly decorated for Christmas. Sean asked at the front desk for Misty's room number and was told she was on the second floor in room 228.

Jacey, Greta and Sean took the elevator up and found Misty's room without difficulty. Sean knocked on the door, pushing it open when Misty's feeble voice beckoned them to come in.

The woman in the hospital bed had a line of sutures along her temple and her left arm was completely bandaged, with pins and rods sticking out of it. The blankets covered her legs, but Jacey assumed the left one was casted, as well. Her heart went out to her fellow trainer.

"Misty? I'm Staff Sergeant Sean Morris and you know Senior Airman Jacey Burke and her K-9 partner, Greta."

"Oh, Misty." Jacey crossed over and lightly rested her hand on Misty's unbroken arm. "I'm so sorry this happened to you."

"Why did you bring a cop?" Misty asked, her gaze full of reproach. "I already told you I didn't go near Greta's kennel."

"Why don't you tell us what you remember about the vehicle that hit you?" Sean countered. "I'm not here to cause trouble. I just want the truth."

Misty reluctantly nodded. "I was waiting at the crosswalk. The sign indicated it was okay to walk, so I did, but a truck zoomed through the intersection, hitting me on the left side." Misty grimaced and tried to shift her position in the bed. "I don't remember anything else until

I woke up here in the hospital. One of the nurses told me that the police would be here to take my statement. But I didn't think you and Jacey would be together."

"I'm so sorry," Jacey repeated. "But Misty, surely you don't think this was an accident? From where I was sitting in the café, it looked as if the truck hit you on purpose."

Misty closed her eyes and turned her head away, as if the news was unbearable. Jacey kept a light grasp on Misty's arm, hoping the physical contact between them would help keep her grounded.

"Misty, did you get a look at the driver?" Sean gently asked.

Misty finally opened her eyes, her lashes wet with tears. "No. I wasn't expecting the truck to be there. I had the walk signal. Did you get a license plate?"

"Unfortunately, the plates were covered with mud," Jacey said. "That's another reason I think it was done on purpose. Whoever hit you didn't want to be identified."

"Why?" Misty asked in an agonized whisper. "Because of Turks?"

"I'm afraid so," Jacey said. "I know you spoke to the journalist Heidi Jenks, as I have. He attacked you, too, didn't he?"

Misty winced and whispered, "Yes."

"How did you get my cell number?"

"From the training-center records," Misty answered. "In fact, I was in your office when I called you."

"My office?" Jacey glanced at Sean, who looked surprised. "Do you use my office often?"

"Sometimes, but only because I don't trust the phone in my office." Misty's voice was getting weaker. "I think someone is spying on me."

Jacey realized Misty may have been the one moving

stuff around in her office. Interesting that they'd both experienced the same sense of being watched, too. Jacey wanted to ask more questions, but Misty's eyelids fluttered closed.

"Come on," Sean said in a low voice. "She needs to rest."

He was right. Misty looked battered, bruised and broken. The best thing they could do for her fellow trainer was to find the person responsible.

They left Misty's hospital room and took the elevator back down to the lobby. "She didn't give us anything to work with," Jacey murmured as they headed outside. "Other than to admit that she was attacked by Turks, too."

"Yeah," Sean agreed. "It's good to have confirmation about Turks. And I think it's interesting that she doesn't trust the cops."

Jacey had noticed that, as well. "Maybe she tried to file a report but was brushed off, the same way Senior Airman Bill Ullman did to me."

"Could be. I'll dig around to see what reports, if any, she filed." Sean placed his hand beneath her elbow. "The jeep is this way."

Sean took extra precautions so they weren't followed, and they made it back to the house without incident. When Jacey took Greta around to the backyard to do her business, Sean tagged along.

"Do you really think Heidi Jenks is in danger?" she asked.

He shrugged. "If the person doing this figures out that she's doing a story on abuse by senior-ranking officers, then yeah, that's a no-brainer."

Jacey shivered and nodded. Bad enough that Misty had been hit by a truck, the thought of adding other innocent victim to the growing list was disturbing to say the least.

"Come, Greta," Jacey called, when it appeared her K-9 was finished. "Let's go inside."

Sean unlocked the back door and held it open for her to precede him inside. In the kitchen, Jacey expected Greta to head straight for her food and water dishes, since the poor thing hadn't finished eating earlier, but instead Greta's nose went up and her entire body quivered.

A chill snaked down Jacey's spine. "Greta?"

The dog lowered her snout to the ground and moved in a zigzag pattern that was achingly familiar. It was the way Greta searched for IEDs in Afghanistan.

"We need to get out of here," she whispered to Sean, but it was too late.

Greta alerted at the stable of the Nativity scene at the same exact moment a man stepped out from behind the Christmas tree.

He was medium height, slim and held a gun. But it wasn't Senior Airman Bill Ullman, as she'd half expected.

It was someone she'd never seen before.

TEN

"Master Sergeant Hanover?" Sean couldn't believe his boss was standing next to the Christmas tree holding a gun on them. "What's going on? Why are you doing this?"

"When you pulled my file, I knew you'd figure it out eventually," the man said in a snide tone. His boss was a few years younger than he was, and Sean had wondered how he'd risen up through the ranks so quickly. Now he knew it wasn't just because Hanover was good. Far from it. Greta stood frozen directly in front of Hanover and he glowered at the animal. "Call off your dog, or I'll shoot it."

"Greta, come," Jacey commanded.

Greta slowly backed up, keeping her dark eyes locked on Hanover.

"What's the link between you and Lieutenant Colonel Turks?" Sean asked, desperate to find a way to protect Jacey. "I mean, it's obvious he's greasing the way for your promotions, and you physically look enough like him to be his son."

Hanover's smile reeked of pure evil and Sean wondered why he hadn't noticed the underlying cruelty before now. "That's exactly why I knew you'd figure it out. You're smart, Morris—I'll give you that. Putting the jeep in my name and then finding this place without going through proper channels. You made me work to find you, that's for sure."

"Are you denying you're related to Lieutenant Colonel Turks?" Sean pressed.

"Not at all. Ivan never bothered to marry my useless mother, and I didn't blame him. It didn't matter, since I'm his son in every way that counts. Having different last names actually worked in our favor. And obviously I'll do whatever is necessary to protect my father." Hanover jerked the weapon toward Jacey. "Tie her up."

Every muscle in Sean's body went tense. He couldn't—wouldn't—allow anything to happen to Jacey.

Liz had died, but he refused to fail again.

"Jacey, run!" Sean shouted at the same time as he heard Jacey tell Greta, "Get him!"

He leaped toward Hanover. The distance was too far, and he braced himself for the gunshot he knew was coming. Greta moved swiftly, clamping her jaw around Hanover's leg.

"Owww!" Hanover fired his weapon and Sean felt the bullet skate along the side of his thigh but ignored the pain. Jacey's panic alarm shrilled loud enough to fracture his eardrums and everyone else's within a ten-mile radius.

Sean took his boss down and Jacey scooped up Hanover's gun. Greta clung to Doug's leg as the guy continued to shriek with pain. At least he appeared to be shrieking; all Sean could hear was the stupid panic alarm.

Finally, Jacey shut it off, the ensuing silence a true blessing.

"Master Sergeant Hanover, you're under arrest for attempted murder," Sean said, slapping handcuffs over his boss's wrists.

"Sean? We better hurry."

"Why?" He glanced up at Jacey, then realized that Greta was sitting straight and tall right next to the stable of the Nativity scene. "Are you saying there's a bomb in there?"

"Yes! Let's go!"

Sean winced as the muscles of his injured thigh protested when he hauled Hanover to his feet. Jacey grabbed Hanover's other arm and they rushed to drag him outside, with Greta keeping pace alongside. Outside, several airmen from nearby houses were milling about, rousted by Jacey's panic alarm.

"All of you, follow us! Hurry!" Sean said. "There's a bomb inside the house!"

Thankfully, the others joined them, and they didn't stop until they were more than halfway down the block.

"We need to call it in," Jacey said between gasping breaths. "Hurry!"

Sean was already fishing his phone out of his pocket when a loud *ka-boom* reverberated through the night.

"The neighbors!" Jacey shouted.

"I live on the west side of the place," one woman said. "My husband is currently overseas."

"We live on the east side," a young couple piped up. "That alarm was crazy loud—I couldn't figure out what was going on!"

Sean managed a smile. "You did it, Jacey. First Greta found the bomb, then that ridiculously loud alarm of yours saved the neighbors."

"We did it," she said. "I didn't even know who he was out of uniform, but you did. I can't believe your boss is Turks's son. And you're bleeding again."

Sean couldn't care less about the wound on his leg. Knowing that Jacey was safe from harm and that he hadn't failed to protect her was all he needed.

Because he loved her.

The realization sank deep into his bones, and he knew that this was the real thing. More than what he'd felt with Liz, although he'd certainly cared about her.

But not the same way he loved Jacey.

He wanted to tell her, to see if she felt even close to the same way, but right now, he needed to stay focused on Hanover. His boss had to pay for his crimes.

"Misty Walsh talked to us just an hour ago," Jacey said, her gaze riveted on Hanover's face. "Between the two of us and any others we can find, we're going to drag your father down off his high-ranking-officer pedestal and toss him in jail where he belongs."

Hanover sneered and swore at Jacey. "You're all alike. Stupid women. You want to do a man's job, but then you're the first to crumble under pressure."

"Assault is not pressure," Jacey shot back.

"Don't waste your breath talking to him," Sean advised. "He's not worth it. Just imagine the two of them sharing a cell, father and son."

Before Jacey could say anything more, additional Special Forces cops arrived, along with half the firetrucks from the apartment fire.

"You again?" The fire chief did not look happy to see them.

"Yes, sir." Sean had to retell their story several times, forced to start over when a superior officer showed up. When Captain Justin Blackwood arrived, he took over the questioning, silencing everyone else.

Hanover tried to interject his side of things, claiming he was being framed and had only come to talk to Sean and Jacey about the case, but thankfully, Jacey had kept his weapon, and handed it over to Captain Blackwood.

"I believe we'll be able to match the ballistics of the bullet Greta found at the parking lot with Hanover's gun," Sean explained.

"Good work, Staff Sergeant," Captain Blackwood said, his expression grim. "I only wish you had escalated this to me sooner."

Sean frowned. "With all due respect, sir, I was keeping my immediate superior up-to-date on my investigation without having any idea he was the one responsible."

"True enough." Justin Blackwood scowled at Hanover. "So, we have Hanover on setting the bomb in the house and two counts of attempted murder. Anything else to add to the list?"

"Three counts of attempted murder, if he drives a black pickup truck," Jacey said. "I saw the truck run the red light and deliberately hit Misty Walsh."

"You can't prove I was the one driving," Hanover protested.

"But I'm sure we'll find traces of Misty's blood and tissue on your truck, won't we?" Sean countered. "Face it—we have you linked to everything."

"I didn't give antifreeze to the dog," Hanover whined.

"Yes, you did." Aiden Gomez stepped out from behind a tree, cradling a pup against his chest. "I saw you at the kennel that night. And Reba admitted to me that she lost her ID. You used it, didn't you?"

"Useless little punk!" Hanover tried to lunge upward, but Sean yanked him back down. "You couldn't have seen me from where you were standing."

Sean couldn't help but smile at how easily Hanover had walked into that one. Apparently being under pressure wasn't working so well for his former boss, either.

"Enough!" Blackwood lifted his hand up. "Hanover, I suggest you exercise your right to keep silent, as anything you say can be used against you in a court-martial. Let's go."

When the Special Forces cops took Hanover away, Sean finally allowed the EMTs to look at his leg. The injury wasn't serious, and only an inch longer than the gash on his arm.

"We'll give you a lift to the ER," the EMT offered.

"No, thanks. Just wrap it up and I'll be fine." The danger was over, but he wasn't about to leave Jacey alone.

The house was gone, her apartment was gone, which left his apartment, if she'd be willing to sleep on the sofa.

Or a motel off base, which didn't really appeal, either.

Then he had a better idea. "How about I take you to Gram's house for the rest of the night?"

"Oh, it's late and I don't want to inconvenience your grandmother," Jacey protested.

"Trust me, we won't be. I have a feeling she'll enjoy meeting the woman who helped bring down a lieutenant colonel."

"I haven't done that yet," she pointed out.

"You will." He had the utmost confidence in her.

"I have Greta, too," she added. "I think it's best if I stay in a motel. A dog-friendly motel."

"Gram loves dogs." He wasn't taking no for an answer. "Will you please trust me on this?"

Jacey hesitated, then nodded. "Okay. I'll trust you. But we'll need to stop by the kennel to pick up additional K-9 supplies. Everything I had in the house is gone."

"Fine with me. Let's go."

Despite it being close to 2200 hours, his grandmother was still up. She opened the door and greeted him with an enthusiastic kiss. "Sean! You're early—I wasn't expecting you until the end of the week!"

"Gram, I'd like you to meet Jacey Burke. Jacey, this is my grandmother, Maureen Morris. We'd like to stay for the night, if that's okay with you."

"Sure, dear," Gram agreed.

"It's so nice to meet you, Ms. Morris. Friend, Greta. Friend." Greta sniffed at Gram, then plopped onto her haunches. "Morris?" Jacey repeated. "Is that your mother's last name?"

"Yes. Thankfully, my stepfather never offered to adopt me."

Gram sighed. "I warned your mother he was no good, but she didn't listen."

Sean kissed her wrinkled cheek. "I know, and I'll always regret how he kept us away from you. But it's okay. Everything worked out just the way God planned."

"Oh, Sean." Gram hugged him close. "I'm glad to hear you say that."

"You can thank Jacey for bringing me back to my faith," he confessed.

Jacey's cheeks turned pink. "I have a feeling you would have come back on your own—I just gave you a gentle nudge."

He wanted so badly to tell her how much he loved her, but before he could think of a way to broach the subject, Jacey continued.

"Ms. Morris, I have to confess, I've had a crush on your grandson ever since high school." Jacey winked at his grandmother. "Despite all the adversity he had to go through, he has turned out to be an exceptional man and an amazing cop."

It was his turn to blush. His grandmother arched a brow.

"I like her, Sean. She's the first woman friend you've

introduced to me and I can see why. Don't mess things up, you hear?" With that Gram turned and walked away. "Good night!" she called over her shoulder.

Jacey chuckled and shook her head. "She's something."

"Yes," he agreed, taking a step closer. "And so are you. I love you, Jacey Burke. If you must know, I had a crush on you back in high school, too."

"Oh, Sean." She slid her arms up and around his neck. "The way you kept pulling away from me, I thought you only liked me as a friend, nothing more."

"Far from it. I was only afraid I'd fail to protect you, the way I failed to protect another woman who I'd promised to protect. She was killed by her ex-husband because I let my guard down. I was convinced I needed to keep you at arm's length to keep you safe." He gazed into Jacey's beautiful deep-brown eyes. "When Hanover held the gun on us, I knew I'd readily sacrifice my life to save you. I love you, Jacey. I know it's fast, and we have barely gone on a proper date, but I hope you're willing to give us a chance."

"Done," she said with a smile. "Because I love you, too." She went up on tiptoe and kissed him.

He cradled her close, his gaze catching the bright star glittering on the top of Gram's Christmas tree. He reveled in her embrace, knowing that God had planned to bring them together all these years later.

For this moment right now.

Jacey had loved spending time with Sean's grandmother, but after three days was grateful to be assigned a new apartment back on base. She decorated the small Christmas tree, the third one, but who was counting? And silently reviewed her many blessings.

First and foremost, Sean. They'd attended Sunday services together and she loved standing beside him in church, listening to his deep baritone as he sang along with the choir. She never felt as close to a man as she did while worshiping God.

Sean filled her in on everything that had taken place when he'd returned to work the morning after the bomb had gone off. Over the next three days, Sean had collected the evidence needed to level charges against Master Sergeant Doug Hanover. When one of Hanover's fingerprints was found inside her old apartment after the fire investigation was complete, the charge of arson was added to the list.

The bullet fragment matched Hanover's gun, and the fingerprint on the dropped bullet was a partial match to him, as well. And a search warrant turned up Reba Pokorny's ID. Sean was happy to have a strong case against Hanover.

Jacey and Misty had renewed their respective formal complaints against Lieutenant Colonel Turks, and Jacey had heard from Heidi that a third female airman had come forward after Heidi's story hit the newspaper. Jacey was convinced even more women would be strong enough to tell their stories, as well, and this time, she was confident that her allegations would be taken seriously and that Turks would stand trial for his crimes, just as Hanover would.

A knock at the door pulled her from her thoughts. Greta let out a quick bark, her tail wagging as she stared at the door. Jacey peered through the peephole to verify Sean was the one standing there.

She unlocked the dead bolt and opened the door. "Hi, you're early."

"I know. Captain Blackwood sent me home and told

me to take the next couple of days off." He swept her into his arms for a long kiss. When he finally came up for air, he added, "I bolted out of there before he could change his mind."

She laughed. "I'm always happy to see you. Check out my Christmas tree. Dinner won't be ready for a while. There's time to relax and make yourself comfy."

"Thanks." He shrugged out of his coat. "By the way, Gram insists on having us over for Christmas brunch. I tried to tell her to let us do the work, but she refused to listen."

"Your grandmother is one stubborn lady," she teased. "I can see where you get it from."

"Me?" His eyes widened with pretend innocence. "You're the most stubborn woman I know."

That made her laugh, but then her smile faded as she caught a glimpse of a snow-globe Christmas ornament that reminded her of Jake. "I'm glad you've invited me to spend the holidays with you," she said with a sad smile. "I only wish Jake could join us."

"I believe he's here, in your heart and in mine," Sean said, pulling her close.

"You're right." She did her best to push her feelings of melancholy away.

"Hey." Sean tipped her face up to meet his gaze. "After everything you've been through, I'm not going to wait until Christmas to give you your present."

"Oh, Sean, I don't need gifts," she protested. "Just being with you is wonderful enough."

His smile broadened. "I was hoping you'd say that."

She tilted her head to the side, confused. Then he slowly dropped down to one knee and held out a small red velvet ring box. Greta wagged her tail, sniffed him, and sat down beside him, but he never took his gaze off

Jacey's. "Jacey Marie Burke, I know it's taken us ten years to find each other again, but now that we have I never want to let you go. Will you please marry me?"

Tears of joy blurred her vision and her heart swelled with love. "Oh, Sean, yes! Yes, I'll marry you." She tugged him to his feet and threw herself into his arms. He caught her close and spun in a small circle. Greta thought it was a game and jumped and barked around them.

He kissed her again, and insisted on sliding the beautiful diamond engagement ring on her finger. Then they stood together staring at the Christmas tree. "Gram is going to be so excited," he said, pressing a kiss against her temple. "She told me not to dawdle in asking you to marry me."

Jacey smiled. "I hardly think a week is exactly dawdling, but I appreciate her concern." She leaned her head against Sean's arm. "I love you so much."

"And I love you, too. Just don't make me wait too long for the ceremony. If Gram has her way, she'll have the whole thing planned before we know it."

"We wouldn't want to disappoint Gram," Jacey agreed. And even though this would be her first Christmas without Jake, she couldn't deny it was already the best Christmas ever.

* * * * *

Dear Reader,

I hope you've enjoyed Sean and Jacey's story. Working on this Military K-9 continuity with such an amazing team of authors has been both an honor and a privilege. I have the utmost respect for the men and women who serve our country, and while I've enjoyed researching the air-force rules and regulations, please excuse any errors as my own.

If you haven't read the entire Military K-9 series, please do so. I promise you won't be disappointed!

I enjoy hearing from my readers so if you're so inclined, stop by my website at www.laurascottbooks.com to drop me a note. Or you can find me on Facebook at Laura Scott Author, or on Twitter @laurascottbooks.

Yours in faith,
Laura Scott

SPECIAL EXCERPT FROM

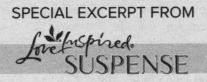

Love Inspired.
SUSPENSE

*With a price on his witness's head,
US marshal Jonathan Mast can think of only
one place to hide Celeste Alexander—in the
Amish community he left behind. But will this trip
home save their lives...and convince them that a
Plain life together is worth fighting for?*

Read on for a sneak preview of
Amish Hideout *by Maggie K. Black,
the exciting beginning to the Amish Witness Protection
miniseries, available January 2019
from Love Inspired Suspense!*

Time was running out for Celeste Alexander. Her fingers flew over the keyboard, knowing each keystroke could be her last before US marshal Jonathan Mast arrived to escort her to her new life in the witness protection program.

"You gave her a laptop?" US marshal Stacy Preston demanded. "Please tell me you didn't let her go online."

"Of course not! She had a basic tablet, with the internet capability disabled." US marshal Karl Adams shot back even before Stacy had finished her sentence.

The battery died. She groaned. Well, that was that.

"You guys mind if I go upstairs and get my charging cable?"

The room went black. Then she heard the distant sound of gunfire erupting outside.

"Get Celeste away from the windows!" Karl shouted. "I'll cover the front."

What was happening? She felt Stacy's strong hand on her arm pulling her out of her chair.

"Come on!" Stacy shouted. "We have to hurry—"

Her voice was swallowed up in the sound of an explosion, expanding and roaring around them, shattering the windows, tossing Celeste backward and engulfing the living room in smoke. Celeste hit the floor, rolled and hit a door frame. She crawled through it, trying to get away from the smoke billowing behind her.

Suddenly a strong hand grabbed her out of the darkness, taking her by the arm and pulling her up to her feet so sharply she stumbled backward into a small room. The door closed behind them. She opened her mouth to scream, but a second hand clamped over her mouth. A flashlight flickered on and she looked up through the smoky haze, past worn blue jeans and a leather jacket, to see the strong lines of a firm jaw trimmed with a black beard, a straight nose and serious eyes staring into hers.

"Celeste Alexander?" He flashed a badge. "I'm Marshal Jonathan Mast. Stay close. I'll keep you safe."

Don't miss
Amish Hideout *by Maggie K. Black,*
available January 2019 wherever
Love Inspired® Suspense books and ebooks are sold.

www.LoveInspired.com

Looking for inspiration in tales
of hope, faith and heartfelt romance?

Check out **Love Inspired**® and
Love Inspired® **Suspense** books!

New books available every month!

CONNECT WITH US AT:

Facebook.com/groups/HarlequinConnection

 Facebook.com/HarlequinBooks

Twitter.com/HarlequinBooks

 Instagram.com/HarlequinBooks

Pinterest.com/HarlequinBooks

ReaderService.com

LIGENRE2018R2

Love Inspired®

Inspirational Romance to Warm Your Heart and Soul

Join our social communities to connect with other readers who share your love!

Sign up for the Love Inspired newsletter at **www.LoveInspired.com** to be the first to find out about upcoming titles, special promotions and exclusive content.

CONNECT WITH US AT:

Facebook.com/groups/HarlequinConnection

 Facebook.com/LoveInspiredBooks

 Twitter.com/LoveInspiredBks

LISOCIAL2018